PRAISE FOR DARRELL PITT

'I found myself laughing out loud which rarely happens.'
Sondra Kerby

'An amazing book that has all the elements
of a great whodunnit.'
Ursula Sorensen

'I'm very much looking forward to reading the next book in
the series.'
Alice Hazelbaker

'This was a fun book to read. It had me laughing
a lot throughout.'
Sandy Mill

' I look forward to future installments.'
Caley Gredig

'What an awesome book!'
Michelle

BY DARRELL PITT

The Boy from Earth
Balloon Girls
A Toaster on Mars

Teen Superheroes
Book I: Diary of a Teenage Superhero
Book II: The Doomsday Device
Book III: The Battle for Earth
Book IV: The Twisted Future
Book V: Terminal Fear
Book VI: The Invisible Weapon
Book VII: The Alpha Project

Teen Superhero Bounty Hunters
Book I: Snakebite
Book II: Fear Fight
Book III: Stormfront
Book IV: Past Shadows
Book V: One Small Step

DARRELL PITT

Cats, Castles and Murder

A ROSIE RYAN COZY MYSTERY

BOOK SEVEN

KENT STREET PRESS

kentstreetpress.com

Copyright © 2023 by Darrell Pitt

This edition published by Kent Street Press, 2025

ISBN: 978-1-923360-38-9 (paperback)

ISBN: 978-1-923360-36-5 (ebook)

A catalogue record of this book is available from the National Library of Australia.

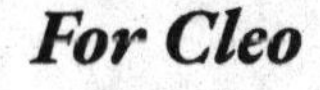

For Cleo

1

'Imagine,' Kim said. 'I could be a movie star!'

'When you're famous,' I said, sighing, 'remember the little people.'

We were sitting out the front of Sandy's Diner in Cape Carson. It was early morning, and Kim had already been for a five-kilometre run. I thought exercise was important, but not so important enough that I had to do anything about it. I'd stayed in bed until a decent hour before making my way down with my beagle, Trixie, to join her for coffee.

'Maybe you could get a role too,' Kim said.

This time I laughed. 'Kim,' I said. 'All I said was that a film company was coming to Cape Carson to make a movie. Other than that, I know nothing! There might not be any roles for anyone.'

'But Rosie—'

I held up a hand. 'Don't forget, I was an entertainment reporter for years,' I said. 'And yes, there are often bit parts, especially when the budget is low. But I know nothing about this film. I don't know who's in it. I don't know the story. It could be about anything.'

'Still…' Kim said wistfully. 'It's always been on my bucket list to appear in a movie. It would be *so* exciting.'

I shrugged. 'It's no big deal.'

Kim stared at me. 'Hang on,' she said. 'Are you say-ing…*you're not saying you've* been in a film? What movie?'

'*Time Rescue*,' I said. 'A sci-fi film. It takes place in the future when the world has been taken over by zombies. I was zombie number 34.'

'Wow,' Kim said. I may as well have told her I was the lead in Sunset Boulevard. 'Was it a speaking part?'

'Only if you count grunts and drooling as speaking. I was in the background. Considering it took them all day to film my scene, they could have used a mannequin instead, and it would have worked as well.'

'Adrian would be impressed if I were in a film,' Kim said.

Adrian Whiteway was Kim's new boyfriend, and I couldn't be happier. He was a lovely guy, good-looking and interesting. He managed an aged care facility in Cape Carson. As the year slid slowly into summer, Kim and Adrian had seen more of each other. I was missing my friend—we'd been spending less time together—but if she was happy, I was too.

'Adrian likes you whether you're a star or not,' I said.

'Maybe. But just imagine—Kim Chen: movie star!'

I gazed out across the sparkling bay. Summer had brought the heat with it, and humidity had produced storms. The good weather days, however, were glorious. The sun rose early, and the skies were a solid sheet of ultramarine blue. Twilight was longer, too, with the days lingering till nine o'clock. When night finally settled, the stars would break out like tiny embers in a fireplace.

I sighed happily. Although our little town of Cape Carson wasn't the centre of the universe, it was close enough for us. Our town on the southern coast of Victoria was as close to paradise as we were likely to get.

Sure, I thought. *We get a few murders, but murders happen everywhere.*

I considered. Actually, we got more than our fair share of murders. Good thing Kim and I were around. Although we were physically different—she was short and I was tall, and she had a strange love of horror and anything ghostly—we were best friends. Together, we'd managed to solve more than a few baffling mysteries along the way.

Trixie whined and cocked her head. Sometimes, I was sure she could read my mind.

I stroked her back. *Yes*, I thought. *And we couldn't do it without you, girl. And the local cops.*

At that moment, a big muscly man came down the road

towards us. Todd Parker, sergeant of the local Cape Carson Police Department, gave us a small wave. He was so large that he barely fit into his police uniform. Although the bad guys may have found him intimidating, I knew he was as gentle as a lamb. And a potential love-interest, though nothing had eventuated as yet.

'Ladies,' he greeted us. 'Mind if I join you?'

We pointed him to a seat. Sandy Clementine, the blond-haired owner of the diner, came out, took his order, and disappeared inside.

'You're out early,' I commented. 'Problems?'

'No more than usual,' Todd sighed, running his hand through his short black hair. 'We've got a few people on holiday, so I got called in to help deal with an early morning disagreement between two neighbours.'

'That doesn't sound too serious.'

'Except it turned into a full-scale fight with one guy hitting the other with a rake.' He rolled his eyes. 'Makes you wish people could at least do us the courtesy of brawling during regular working hours.'

Sandy came out with Todd's coffee and scooted away.

'It's most inconsiderate of them,' I agreed. 'You got much else on for the day?'

'I hope not. If cops can have holidays, why can't the crims?'

Kim leaned forward. 'Have you heard about the movie?'

'Cat Burglar?'

'Is that what it's called?' I asked.

Todd took a long sip of his black coffee. 'Can you girls keep a secret?'

'What a silly question!' I said. 'We have impeccable morals!'

'Really?' Todd pulled a face. 'Do I need to mention how many times you've broken the law? And you seem to stumble across dead bodies at an alarming rate?'

'People keep leaving them about,' Kim said.

'We can't help if we fall over them,' I agreed. 'Killers should tidy up after themselves.'

'Anyway,' Todd continued, 'the name of the movie is Cat Burglar, and I've already received a threatening message about the movie.'

'Really, Todd?' My journalistic senses began to tingle. 'Threatening what?'

'That it shouldn't go ahead. Whoever sent it said they'd do everything possible to close down production.'

'It's hard to imagine that anyone would be against the idea.' The movie would bring badly needed money into the area and put Cape Carson on the map. 'They didn't say why they hated the film?'

'No, *and* they didn't identify themselves either.'

'If they had,' Kim said, 'it might have made life much easier.' She glanced at her watch. 'I'd better get moving. We've got a girl away on holiday this week too.'

Kim was in charge of the local library. She said goodbye and left as I went inside to pay. By the time I returned, Todd was already on the footpath, staring wistfully at the bay. I collected Trixie and joined him.

'It's a nice day out there,' I said.

Todd nodded without speaking.

'Okay,' I said. 'What is it?'

'Huh?'

'I can tell when you've got something on your mind.'

The big man shrugged. Sometimes, for someone so large, he looked incredibly boyish, and that's how he looked now.

'It's this movie,' he said, his mouth turning down. 'The director is Laura Gleep.'

'Oh, yes,' I said. 'I know her.'

'Really?'

Now it was my turn to eye-roll. 'Try not to look so amazed. I did have a life before Cape Carson.' I looked at him closer. 'Wait a minute. You were a child actor. You didn't work with Laura...'

He nodded. 'I'm afraid so,' he said. 'She directed a season of Rusty Jones.'

Several years of Todd's childhood had been taken up with him starring in The Rusty Jones Mysteries. Those days were not happy memories for Todd. His father had pushed his career, and kids at school had bullied him. His time in the mystery series had led to Todd becoming both a cop and a bodybuilder.

'And I suppose she'll remember you,' I said.

'Yes.' Todd looked glum. 'I hate being reminded of all that stuff.'

'It can't have been all bad.'

'No, but sometimes the past is best left behind.'

Although I wanted to get to work early, there were times when friends took precedence. 'Feel like a walk?' I suggested. 'I've got time to kill.'

He glanced at his watch. 'Why not? It's a nice day.'

We headed down to the beach and followed the coastal path up to the lighthouse. Here, we lingered under the monolith and stared out at the ocean. Despite summer having only just begun, the media was already full of stories about Christmas. Unlike the Northern hemisphere, Christmas in Australia took place in the middle of summer. Christmas Day could be one of the hottest days of the year.

'Do you know what's happening with the Unicorn Bookstore?' I asked. The bookshop had closed recently and was in want of a new owner.

'Only that it might be reopening soon.'

'Really?' My interest was piqued. 'Feel like taking a look?'

He agreed, and we headed up to Third Avenue, where the

old Georgian-style building sat. It had been one of the busiest places in town until recently. Now it sat vacant and unloved. I stared closer. The real estate sign across the front now had a *SOLD* sticker plastered across it.

'Ah-ha,' I said. 'You were right. So it could be reopening soon.'

'It wasn't listed with your daughter Amanda?' Todd asked.

Amanda and her husband, Tom Healy, owned one of the town's most successful real estate businesses. 'No. It was with Carson Realty.' That was their chief competition. 'Hope it stays as a bookshop.'

Todd's phone buzzed, and he glanced at it. 'I'd better get going,' he said. 'Duty calls.' He smiled. 'Thanks for the walk.'

'No worries. Any time.'

Wishing him a good day, Trixie and I watched as he headed off. I turned my attention back to the old building.

Hmm, I thought. *Who could be the new owner?*

2

'I have arrived!' I announced loudly.

'So I noticed,' Doris Glow said. The Cape Carson Gazette's receptionist glanced up from her desk. She peered more closely at me. 'And you've got bacon and eggs on your shirt.'

'Oh bother!'

She was right.

I was a woman of many skills, with clumsiness being one of them. After returning home, my grandmother—Nan to everyone—had quickly thrown together some breakfast. It looked like I'd just as quickly tossed some onto my shirt and not noticed before leaving the house. As I dabbed it off with a tissue, the editor of the Gazette, Harry Blackshore, yelled out to me.

'Rosie!' he said. 'Are you busy?'

'Only cleaning my shirt.'

'That's a waste of time. Everyone knows you're not house-trained.'

I leaned into his office. 'Okay, Mister Smarty-Pants,' I groaned. 'What's up?'

'That's what I like to hear. A tone of reverence for your boss. Grab a seat.'

I sat.

'You know Alex Carlyle?' Harry asked.

'Unfortunately—yes.'

The millionaire was a notorious recluse living in one of Victoria's only castles. Carlyle Castle—as he modestly christened it—was located about fifty kilometres north of Cape Carson. Although I'd seen photos of it, I'd never visited the property. One reason was that I'd never been invited. The other was that Alex Carlyle was known as one of the nastiest people to ever walk the earth.

I continued. 'You're not about to give me some good news?' I said. 'That Alex Carlyle is dead? Because if you are...'

'No such luck,' Harry said, laughing. 'Yes, I know he's a cantankerous old man. I don't know anyone who's ever had anything good to say about him. But something's come up that I think you'll be interested in. And besides,' he paused, 'Alex has asked for you.'

I stared at him blankly. 'Alex Carlyle has asked for me?' I said. 'You mean...what do you mean? Harry, I once had a run-in with that horrible old buzzard. Alex tried to pull into a parking spot as I tried to reverse into it. He was driving that huge grey Mercedes of his. I narrowly avoided crashing into him. I jumped out yelling, and so did he.'

I thought back to the incident.

He'd called me a terrible driver and my Flame Red 2005 Jeep Wrangler Unlimited Rubicon a pile of junk. I'd given as good as he'd given, though. In the end, a passer-by intervened, and I'd reluctantly surrendered the parking spot to him. I hadn't forgotten the incident, and he hadn't either. Three days after the disagreement, a parcel arrived at the office for me. Opening it with some trepidation, a glitter bomb had exploded, showering me with tiny tinsel that had taken a week to get out of my hair. While I usually would have appreciated the humour of such a thing, I also discovered a tiny model of a red Jeep Wrangler—crushed—at the bottom of the parcel. There was no note. Nothing. No indication as to the sender.

Except, I knew exactly who it was from: Alex Carlyle. It was a practical joke laced with a dose of nastiness.

'Why does he want to see me?' I now asked Harry. 'If he wants a fight—'

'He's donating ten million dollars to the hospital.'

'Huh?'

'You heard me. Alex Carlyle is donating ten million to Cape Carson hospital. It's to help build the new children's ward.'

That made no sense. Not that people wouldn't want to help a hospital. *That* made sense. What didn't make sense was that *Alex Carlyle* would do so. He was renowned for being as ruthless in his private dealings as in his business relationships. No one had anything good to say about him. The best that could be said was that he was successful. Hated but successful.

Which was why a donation to the local hospital made no sense. I'd never heard of him donating money to anything or anyone. His whole life had been money, money, money, and gathering it all for himself.

'And what does he want?' I asked.

Harry raised an eyebrow. 'What do you mean?'

'He does nothing for anyone. Seriously, Alex Carlyle is a terrible person. Why is he suddenly donating a huge sum to our local hospital?'

'I have no idea, and it's your job to find out.'

'He rang you?'

'His butler rang me.'

Butler?

I groaned internally. Well, I suppose people in Alex Carlyle's position had butlers.

'Alex has specifically invited you to his castle this weekend,' Harry continued. 'He's holding a family gathering and would like you there.'

'So he can mock me in front of everyone or...'

'He wants you to write the story.'

'I see.' Mostly I was prepared to bend to Harry's wishes, but not this time. I had no desire to be in the firing line of Alex Carlyle's taunts. And holed up in his huge castle surrounded by his family sounded like a great way to make an utter fool of myself. 'Thanks,' I told Harry. 'But—no thanks.'

'If you refuse, he won't donate the money to the hospital.'

'What?'

'It's true.' Harry shrugged. 'I know it's crazy. But that's what the butler—Elliot Tyson—told me. No Rosie: no money.'

'That's insane!' I snapped. 'How crazy is that old buzzard?'

'Pretty crazy,' Harry agreed, sighing. 'Rosie, it's up to you. It's your call. You can say *no* if you want.'

You can say no if you want.

Yes, I could say *no*, and that's what I wanted to do. I'd never had much time for nasty people. But I had ten million reasons to say *yes*. The real question was—why did he want *me* there? Why me, of all people? To mock me? To make a point? Or was he so enamoured with my reporting skills that he truly believed I was the best person to write about his donation?

Regardless, there could really only be one answer.

'Okay,' I said reluctantly. 'I'll do it.'

3

I spent the next few hours finishing up stories I'd been working on for the last few days. These included yet another development proposal from local businessman Giuseppe Costa to redevelop West beach. He was another local businessman with whom I'd had more than a few run-ins. The council, thank goodness, had declined his development application, and I hoped it would never go ahead.

Heading up the road for lunch, I took Trixie with me and ended up back at Sandy's Diner. After polishing off a burger, chips, and a soft drink, Sandy somehow talked me into an additional slice of apple and walnut cake.

'It's low fat,' Sandy told me, somehow keeping a straight face.

'So's water,' I told her. 'All right. One slice—but make it small.'

'Aye, aye, Captain.'

She disappeared inside while I pulled out my phone and

brought up some information about Alex Carlyle. Sandy brought out my meal, and I ate slowly while reading my phone. Half an hour later, I'd finished my lunch and knew more about Alex Carlyle than I'd ever known before. Still, the more I learned, the less I felt I knew. There was a mystery about the man. If I hadn't had my run-in with him over that parking space, I would have eventually sought him out for an interview.

His father—Craig Carlyle—had migrated to Australia from Scotland with only the clothes on his back. He'd worked in a grocery store. His other talent was that he knew how to work—and wasn't afraid to do so. Working seven days a week, Craig had immediately gone about starting a grocery store in the heart of Melbourne. One shop had led to another, and before long, the man had built an empire under the name of Carlyle Groceries.

This was the world in which Alex Caryle had grown up. His father had taught him everything he knew until fate struck a cruel blow. One day, while changing a light bulb over a high set of stairs, the old man fell and died from a fractured skull. Alex's mother died soon after from cancer.

Alex Carlyle had inherited everything, including his father's work ethic. Working seven days a week, the empire had grown. Along the way, Alex had somehow found the time to meet a woman, marry and sire three children. From all reports, however, it sounded like his relationship with his children had been problematic.

The media was full of stories about all three children suffering failed businesses and facing numerous financial issues.

Carlyle Groceries had eventually become one of Australia's most successful chain of small grocery stores. A game-changer for the firm had been an inventory system that automatically reordered stock. The inventory system—Wishart—had been on-sold to other companies, including an independent chain in the UK and another in America. This had brought in countless millions for the company.

All this success had not brought happiness for Alex Carlyle. His wife had died during a botched home invasion while Alex was away on business. Over the years, a series of heart attacks forced the old man into early retirement. This was when he turned his attention to the construction of Carlyle Castle.

Alex Carlyle had become notoriously reclusive, although he wasn't a shut-in. He wasn't afraid to go out and—as was my experience—yell at the locals. Alex simply preferred to stay in the castle like a king looking out over his royal subjects.

Mind you, none of us thought of him as his subjects. Most of us even considered a castle in the Australian countryside vaguely ridiculous. Castles were fine in the United Kingdom or Europe, but here—

'Hey Rosie.'

I glanced up to see my ex-husband George approaching with Amanda. George was looking good these days, better than he had in years. For some time, he'd been unhealthy and turning to fat. Now a lot of that fat had been worn away since he'd started dating a woman named Sadie Brielle. George pushed back his short brown hair and smiled as he sat down.

Amanda looked happy too. She was married and looked like me—tall with longish brown hair and eyes—although she wasn't carrying ten kilos of middle-aged fat.

'Hello, you two,' I said.

'You working, mum?' Amanda asked as she sat.

'Doing some research for a story.'

'Got a minute?' George asked.

'Sure.'

I was worried. I didn't often see Amanda out with her father, and this had all the elements of an ambush. *Okay*, I thought. *What's going on?* Although Amanda looked relaxed, George's face was a little pensive.

'What's up?' I asked. 'Is everything okay?'

'Everything's fine,' Amanda said. 'Dad's got some news.'

'Really?' I turned to him. 'George?'

'It's nothing, really,' George said, reddening. 'Well, it is, I suppose. But it's about Sadie. And me.'

'Is she okay?' And then I knew: it struck me like a tonne of bricks. 'You're getting married.'

'Yes.' George gave me an embarrassed smile. 'We are.'

Married.

'Wow,' I said. 'That's...amazing. Fantastic. Such good news. Sadie's a lovely person. I'm...' I was at a complete loss as to how to continue. 'You'll be very happy.'

George and Amanda continued to speak, and I somehow managed to ask if a date had been set for the wedding. It hadn't, but I barely heard the answer. My heart was thudding hard, and I felt lightheaded. I glanced at my watch.

'Wow,' I said. 'I'd better go. I've got an interview happening.'

'We'll talk later?' Amanda said.

'Sure. Fantastic.'

I went inside and paid up before collecting Trixie and giving them a wave. They both looked calm and happy, and somehow I managed to project the same demeanour. I headed for the office but kept going and reached Cut Rock Lookout a few minutes later. I was lucky, and no one was about.

I burst into tears.

The weirdest thing was that I wasn't even sure *why* I was crying. It was like my body had been taken over by an outside force. As if gravity had suddenly flipped upside-down. After a few minutes, I took out my phone and rang Kim. She was my go-to person whenever catastrophe struck. Actually, she was my go-to person for pretty much anything.

She listened sympathetically as I told her George's news.

'So I'm sitting here at the lookout,' I said. 'And bawling my eyes out—and I don't know why.'

'It's shock,' she said. 'And change can seem difficult. It's the end of something. A *permanent* end.'

That's one of the things I loved most about Kim. She somehow managed to simultaneously be the ditsiest person I'd ever known and also the smartest.

'But George and I haven't been together for years,' I pointed out. 'I'm not in love with him. I mean, I *love* him, but not *in love*.'

'I know what you mean. It'll take time to process. It's only in the movies where stuff gets settled from one scene to the next. In real life, it takes days and weeks, and sometimes *years* to come to terms with things.'

'I suppose that's true.' I thought. 'And like you say, change is hard.'

'Hmm, I'm not saying change *has* to be hard. It's all how we look at it. You're not eighteen anymore. A lot of water's passed under the bridge. You've moved on, and so has he. And at least Sadie's a good person.'

'Kim,' I sighed. 'How is it that you're so smart?'

'I'm a librarian. All librarians are smart.'

'If you say so.' I looked at my watch. 'Look, I've really got to get going. I'm meeting with Laura Gleep about her movie.'

'Oh! Great! Don't forget about getting a role for me! It

doesn't need to be a speaking role. I'd be happy in the background. Not too much in the background—'

Warning Kim not to hold her breath, I thanked her and hung up. Soon, I was driving over to the old sports centre on Third Avenue. It was only a few hundred metres up the road from the Unicorn bookstore. The sports centre had been closed for years after the new place was built. Now the derelict building was a hive of activity, with vans parked out the front and people pouring in and out through the main door.

'Wow,' I said to Trixie. 'This production really has brought some business to Cape Carson.'

She gave a happy bark.

We continued inside. The building had previously hosted basketball, netball, and indoor soccer games. The vast pavilion had been subdivided into various sets. At a glance, I could make out a faux living room, kitchen, and what appeared to be the interior of a warehouse. Through the wonders of filmmaking, I knew the director would insert some exterior shots and stitch them all together to make the film. People were everywhere, and I wondered if I'd even recognise Laura Gleep. Then I heard—

'Rosie Ryan!'

The woman emerged from the crowd and strode towards me. It was like watching the parting of the waves. Laura was even taller than me and wore a flowing gossamer gown and bejewelled knit turban.

'Darling!' she declared the word so loudly that it probably registered on the Richter scale. 'Imagine finding you here! Hiding in this little corner of the world of all places!'

'Laura.' I tried to hide my irritation. I wasn't hiding anywhere, and I didn't appreciate anyone regarding Cape Carson as a little corner of anything. 'It's been a while.'

'My goodness. A while. Let me see, was it at the Logie's afterparty? It must have been. You remember when Danny Dunkle drank that bottle of champagne and collapsed on top of Gloria Swain? Tore her dress in two! My goodness! What a scene!'

It may have been quite a scene, but it wasn't one I was privy to. Actually, I didn't know Gloria Swain, and all I knew of Danny Dunkle was that he was currently serving time in prison for drunk driving.

'Ah, the parties...the parties,' she continued, lost in the reverie of her own history. 'And here we are now. Another movie. Another location. My goodness. The crazy world of filmmaking. It's a fickle business.' Her eyes narrowed on me. 'What is it?'

With a growing sense of dismay, I recalled one of Laura's least endearing traits. She had this annoying habit of saying something and then testing you on it to see if you were listening.

'Fickle?' I repeated faintly.

'Fickle! That's right! Fickle!' She spat the words at me as if the uncertain world of filmmaking was completely my fault. 'But you know who survives? Those that work. Those who seek opportunities and take them!' She clenched her fist as if planning an invasion of Europe and not making a movie. 'That's what sets us apart, Rosie. We work. We strive. We take chances, and sometimes we have to accept less than the best.' Upon saying this, she placed a firm hand on my shoulder. 'We all have falls from grace.'

I got the impression she thought my move to Cape Carson was like landing in a garbage bin. 'I'm very happy where I am,' I said, gently shrugging off her hand. 'This is a wonderful town—'

'I'm sure it is. Finding a good coffee must be a trial—'

'Actually, there's plenty of good coffee—'

'—but life isn't all about coffee,' she concluded. 'There's work, and that's what matters.'

'Yes. Well, anyway, tell me about your movie,' I said, seizing the opportunity. 'It's called *Cat Burglar*?'

Just as Laura opened her mouth to answer, her eyes opened, and she looked past me. 'My goodness,' she muttered. 'Is that a hunk of man or what?'

I glanced back to see that Todd Parker had just entered. This was when I remembered another of Laura's less endearing traits. She was a terrible man-chaser. In fact, she was the only person I personally knew who'd been married seven times. One marriage lasted only three days. Laura had once declared in an interview that marriage was like dating but with a prenup attached.

Goodness, I thought. *Poor Todd's become bait, and he doesn't know it.*

After I'd introduced Todd to Laura, he told her the purpose of his visit and asked if we could find somewhere to speak in private.

'Do you mind if I tag along?' I asked.

Before Todd could reply, Laura laughed. 'Of course, Rosie,' she said. 'The more the merrier!'

There were a dozen trailers jammed in behind the sports centre. Soon, we were sitting in her trailer. It was a cramped space, but not as bad as some I've been in.

'We've received a threat about the movie,' Todd began. 'Cat Burglar.'

Laura rolled her eyes. 'There are always malcontents around,' she said. 'People who oppose the creative arts, who think art has no place in modern society.' Her eyes narrowed on the bulky policeman. 'Wait a minute. Wait a minute! Todd Parker! Of course. The Rusty Jones Mysteries!'

Todd swallowed. 'Oh yes,' he said airily. 'That was a long time back. Now, if we can get back to the issue at hand—'

'So you're a policeman now,' Laura continued. She gave me a wink so big you could have seen it in New Zealand. 'A *very* grown-up policeman. Hubba-hubba! Now, don't you worry about anything, Todd darling. I get threats all the time. It comes with the territory.'

'This threat isn't directed at you,' Todd said. 'The note specifically mentions a Mrs Charles by name. Can we see her, please? Is she around?'

A tiny frown crossed Laura's brow. 'Well,' she said, taken aback. 'Of course.' She raised her voice. 'Tina! Tina! Where is that girl? She's never around when I need her!'

'And Tina is...' I prompted.

'My personal assistant.'

A thin, black-haired girl who looked like she'd come straight from a goth concert stepped into the van. 'Yes, Laura?' she said.

'This policeman would like to see Mrs Charles.'

Tina nodded and disappeared.

A few minutes passed as we waited. Then a skinny woman with slightly bucked teeth and square glasses appeared in the doorway. Nestled in her arms was a black and white American shorthair cat.

She eased herself into the trailer, giving us a quizzical look. 'Yes, Laura?' she said. 'You wanted to see me?'

Laura Gleep introduced us.

'Mrs Charles,' Todd said. 'I'm afraid we've had a threat made against your life.'

'What?' The woman's jaw dropped. 'No! That's terrible!' She gripped her cat a little tighter. 'What monster would threaten my little Charlie-Warley?'

4

It took a moment for this to sink in.

'*Mrs Charles is your cat?*' I said. 'And you are?'

The woman looked close to tears. 'Monica Crumb,' the woman said. 'Her beloved owner.'

Laura Gleep turned to us. 'Mrs Charles is the star of Cat Burglar,' she said.

Which was as clear as mud.

'Okay,' Todd said slowly. 'The star of the film *is a cat*? This cat?'

'All the actors in *Cat Burglar* are cats,' Laura explained. 'It's an entirely feline cast.'

By now, I had my notebook out. 'The whole cast?' I said. 'All cats?'

'Indeed. It's the first movie of its kind in Australia. Possibly the world.'

Todd was frowning. 'So someone's threatened the life of...Mrs Charles,' he said to Monica. 'Why would someone want to harm your cat?'

'Stars are always being threatened,' Laura broke in. 'Rosie knows all about that.'

'I do?' I said. 'Oh, well, I suppose that's true.' There were stalkers out there who threatened celebrities. 'But these are cats. Why would someone—'

Monica leaned close. 'Mrs Charles will be the most famous cat in the world when *Cat Burglar* is released,' she said. 'She already has her own website, and we have several products in development.'

'I see,' I said, although I didn't see at all.

'Plus her autobiography.'

Todd and I exchanged glances.

'Her autobiography?' Todd said, finally. 'How—'

'I helped write it,' Monica admitted. 'She's busy with her career.'

This was getting us nowhere. 'Can you tell us a bit more about the movie?' I asked Laura.

'Of course, Rosie.' Laura beamed brightly. 'This is a *big* movie, darling. *Enormous!* A feline film with our feline friends, dressed to kill. We expect the fashions alone will take the world by storm.'

'The fashions?' I said.

'The cats will be dressed. We've even invented a name that we're hoping will trend.' She paused dramatically. '*Apurral.*'

I stared at her. 'The cats will be wearing clothing?'

'What else, darling?' Laura gave me a bemused look. '*Apurral*! It's got quite a ring to it. Don't you think?'

Todd asked, 'Does this movie have a story?'

'Of course, darling!' She framed an imaginary cinema screen with her hands. '*Cat Burglar* is about a female cat—Delilah Claw—who has lived alone as a thief all her life. Then she meets the man—er—cat of her dreams, Sam Whiskers. But here's the conflict: Sam's a detective with the police department. His job is to bring her to justice, and her job is to elude him. Can she give up a life of pilfering in the name of love? Or will they forever remain on opposite sides of the law?'

And will anyone want to watch this movie? I wondered. *It sounds like the oldest plot in the world—but with cats.*

I suppose they save money on paying real actors.

'At present,' Laura said, 'we only have the three leading cats on set. After their scenes are filmed, we'll be bringing in the extras to complete the film.'

'None of this explains why someone would threaten...er, Mrs Charles,' Todd said to her. 'Have you received any threats?'

Laura faltered. 'Not at all,' she said. 'Everyone's on board.'

I sensed that she was lying but could hardly accuse her. Todd's eyes had narrowed too. Just as he seemed ready to say more, a young woman, who looked like a younger version of

Monica, appeared in the doorway.

'Mum?' she said.

'It's nothing,' Monica said to her. 'Sergeant and Rosie, this is my daughter, Elisa.'

Elisa's eyes slid to Trixie. 'Your dog is very well-behaved,' she said, her voice almost mouselike. 'She likes cats?'

'Trixie likes everyone,' I said. 'Or almost everyone.'

Before I could continue, Laura grabbed up a folder jammed with paper. 'That's all very lovely,' she said. 'But time waits for no man—or woman, as is the case. This is our press kit.' She pushed it into my hands. 'Everything you need to know is in here. Now, come and I'll introduce you around.'

Todd and I spent the next half an hour in a series of whirlwind introductions.

As it was impossible to interview everyone, we decided to focus on the owners of the other cats in the film. Egomania on film sets went with the territory. First, there was Sandra Shelby, the owner of Bob, a red Persian. The woman was forty with a Rubenesque figure and a vast head of curly hair. Her cat, Bob, played the movie's detective, Sam Whiskers.

'Mrs Charles has been threatened?' Sandra said, her mouth opening wide. 'Good heavens! Who would do such a terrible thing?'

'That's what we're trying to find out,' Todd replied.

'Although,' Sandra added thoughtfully, 'as one door closes,

another opens. If something happened to darling Mrs Charles, then another puss would need to fill her shoes, or boots.' She laughed. 'Puss in boots!'

I frowned. 'And that could be Bob?' I said. 'But Bob is male.'

'No one need notice. Wonderful things can be done with camera angles.' She sighed. 'You must think I'm terrible. I don't want anything awful to happen to Mrs Charles. She's an adorable cat. Just not as active as a cat can be. That's all I'm saying.'

I was sure she was saying a lot more than that, but Todd and I left her and continued on to find Gerry Baxter. His cat, Terry, an Abyssinian, was playing the detective's sidekick, Terry Pawson. Gerry was a pleasant-looking man with big ears and a goofy grin. He seemed to always be smiling, even when he wasn't.

'That's terrible about Mrs Charles,' he said as we stood behind one of the trailers. With his perpetually smiling face, Gerry didn't look disappointed. He stroked his cat lovingly. 'Simply awful.'

'Of course,' Todd said, 'if anything were to happen to Mrs Charles, another cat would take her role.'

'I suppose so,' Gerry said. 'Although it's not an easy role to cast.'

'It's not?' I said.

'These can be demanding roles. A cat must be lively and

responsive and enjoy dressing up. Not all cats do.'

I'd never thought much about dressing up animals. I was about to ask him about it when—

'Heavens! It's Rosie Ryan!'

I knew that voice all too well. Todd and I turned to see the mayor of Cape Carson, Regina Lynch. A slim woman in her fifties, her hair was worn in a blonde bob. She came scurrying over.

'And Cape Carson's finest!' Regina continued.

'Regina,' Todd greeted her.

'And little Trixie!'

Trixie yowled.

Gerry seized the opportunity to escape and wished us all a good day.

'I'm so glad I've caught you here,' Regina said. 'Especially you, Rosie.'

'Why?' I asked suspiciously.

'You're an influential person! One of Cape Carson's most famous celebrities! A woman who knows people.'

'Huh?'

'Of course.' She patted my arm gently and turned to Todd. 'Everyone *loves* Rosie. There could be a TV show with that name: *Everyone Loves Rosie*! My goodness!'

Oh sure, I thought. *A TV show about me.*

Regina Lynch wasn't mayor for no reason at all. She always

made a point of being seen in all the right places and with all the right people. More than anything else, everything she did was to advance her own career.

Todd seemed to be having the same thought. 'I've done all I can here,' he said. 'Better get moving.'

I glared at him, and the slightest smile played on his lips.

You rotter! I thought. *Leaving me here with this awful woman!*

He left, and I turned to Regina. 'What can I help you with?' I asked.

'It's this movie,' Regina said. 'And Buttercup.'

'Buttercup?'

'My cat. Buttercup's a Russian Blue. *An exquisite creature!* And so well-natured.' She paused. 'I'm absolutely certain that stardom awaits.'

'Okay.'

I had no idea what this had to do with me.

Regina continued. 'I know you and Laura are old friends,' she said. 'There must be a role for Buttercup in this film. Not a big part. But surely a speaking part—'

'It's a cat film,' I said flatly. 'There are no speaking parts.'

'They're dubbing the voices in later.'

'Oh,' I said. That's how it was being done. Regina seemed to know more about this movie than me. 'But Laura and I aren't old friends. I interviewed her a few years back. That's all.'

The mayor laughed loudly. 'Oh, Rosie!' she said. 'But Laura will *listen* to you. She'll take your advice. I've tried speaking to her, and she shut me down. Laura obviously doesn't know how people feel about me in Cape Carson. Although I don't think of myself as a celebrity, many people do. You simply must convince her that having Buttercup will make Cat Burglar a stunning success!'

There were so many preposterous things in this statement that it was hard to respond. Finally, I said, 'I'll do what I can,' and wished her a good day.

The hive of activity around the sports centre had increased by the time I reached the car with Trixie. The production appeared to be on a tight schedule. Nothing was surprising about that. Movie sets were either all go or nothing at all.

My phone rang.

'Harry?' I answered.

'I've got half an empty page to fill,' he said. 'I'm hoping you can help me out. Otherwise I'm adding *Interesting Places* back into the paper—and you know how much I hate that.'

Interesting Places was a series of filler articles he'd written in case we desperately needed to fill a hole in the paper. Even I had to admit it was not Harry's best work. It was essentially a series of local history profiles of places that—sadly—were not that interesting.

And we were going to press today. It had slipped my mind

amid the day's craziness. I glanced down at the clutch of press materials in my hand. 'Never fear,' I said. 'Rosie is here. I'll have that gap filled before you know it.'

5

'What a day!' I groaned as I dumped myself and my handbag onto the couch.

'Busy?' Nan asked, grating mozzarella in our kitchen.

'More than busy. Frantic!'

Nan was my grandmother, and although her name was Nancy, everyone in the world knew her as Nan. I allowed myself a brief minute of respite before I got up and helped to make dinner.

Although she was the sprightliest and sassiest eighty-something year old that I'd ever known, she wasn't getting any younger. Homemade pizza was on the menu for tonight; sharing the house with her meant I shared at least half the chores.

She listened silently as I sprinkled topping onto the pizza and told her the day's events. Nan nodded. 'Alex Carlyle,' she said. 'I remember you telling me about the incident with the parking space.'

'He's a rude, horrible old man.'

Nan didn't speak for a moment. 'He wasn't always like that,' she said. 'We dated when we were young.'

I laughed—then saw the look on her face. 'You're kidding.'

'Not at all. Alex was a goodlooking man. Had a sense of humour, too.'

'We're talking about the same Alex Carlyle? The tyrant of Carlyle Castle?'

Nan gave a gentle laugh. 'The one and the same.'

'Then you're the only person who thinks of him as human. The rest of the world sees him as the local despot.'

'Life changes people,' Nan said. 'His father was a tough, brutal man. All business. No fun. Craig Carlyle worked seven days a week, and eventually, so did Alex. At one time...'

I stared at her. 'What?'

'Nothing. It's just that I was seeing two men at the time. Nothing serious, mind you. I was single and allowed to date whomever I wanted. One of the men was Alex, and the other was Frank.'

Frank Ryan was my grandfather. My eyes angled to a painting on the wall of him. Then I realised what Nan was really saying.

'You could have married Alex?' I said. 'Really?'

She shrugged. 'If things had been different.'

'So what happened?'

'Frank decided to pursue me while Alex decided to chase

money. Alex Carlyle got what he wanted.' She smiled. 'And so did I. Rosie, your grandfather was the finest man I ever knew. Every day was a blessing. Believe me. I don't regret the choices I made for a single second.'

Still, as I slid the pizza into the oven, I thought about how things could have been different. If Nan had continued to date Alex, then he could have been...

Good grief, I thought. *He could have been my grandfather!*

I tried not to overthink this as I ate dinner with Nan. There were things you didn't want to dwell on, and that was one of them. I ended up having an early night. The following day Nan was heading out with her boyfriend, Dave, to visit a vintage car show.

As for me, I spent the day relaxing before finally heading off to Carlyle Castle. The drive to the castle took around an hour. The road was winding, and the countryside hot and dry.

I finally reached the entrance to the estate, a narrow road that pushed through an overgrown pine tree forest.

After following this for a few minutes, I manoeuvred my jeep around a series of sharp turns before cresting a hill and catching my first look at Carlyle Castle.

It was both the same and different from what I'd seen in photos. It was a big squarish hulk, with turrets at each corner and a moat adjoining the building. A field surrounded the property on all sides, bordered by pines.

Trixie whined at the sight of the unfamiliar building.

'It's okay, girl,' I said, patting her. 'There are no archers up there or people wanting to pour boiling water on us.' I thought about Alex Carlyle. 'Well, I don't think there is.'

As I reached the drawbridge across the moat, I slowed the car. Now that I was here, I felt a mixture of excitement and silliness.

I'd been to the United Kingdom and visited real castles. They were a sight to behold. This was a pretend building. At the same time, there was a thrill in seeing the place up close. There was no denying it. Carlyle Castle was impressive, if only for its size. The walls stretched fifty feet above the ground, and although the moat wasn't wide—only about twenty feet across—it looked murky and deep.

The bridge did not draw back; it was permanent. A draw-bridge would have created a formidable form of defence if this were a real castle. I trundled across the bridge in my jeep into the courtyard beyond. Two other cars were already here. A grey Mercedes—Alex Carlyle's car—an old Holden, and a jeep.

Beyond the courtyard lay the keep, apparently attached to the rear curtain wall and running most of the length of the courtyard. Jutting against one end was a rather incongruous timber building that I realised was a garage.

Many stone keep castles would have a curtain wall surrounding the entire structure, with the keep standing alone, a last impenetrable barrier to defend the castle owner. Once the outer perimeter was breached, the attackers entered the bailey, or courtyard, where I stood.

The windows on the building were relatively modern. Big square things designed to allow in air and light with timber frames. This place was part castle and part manor house.

The front door eased open as if by magic and I was confronted by a man in a tuxedo. At first, I thought I'd arrived in the middle of a dinner party. Then my mind went to the rather more obvious explanation: this was the butler.

'Hello?' I hazarded.

'Miss Ryan?' he said, his voice deep and resonant.

I stepped closer. He was over six feet tall, gaunt, and pale with thinning hair. The overall impression was one of Lurch from the Addams Family.

'Rosie,' I said. 'Rosie Ryan.'

'I am Elliot,' he said. 'Mister Carlyle's butler. You've come for the weekend.'

Although he said it as a statement, it may as well have been a question. 'Yes,' I said. 'I've been invited.'

'Mister Carlyle's son, Simon, has already arrived. You're the second guest to arrive.'

I nodded.

'Do you have bags?' he asked.

'Just one.'

He waited.

I crossed wordlessly to my car, retrieved it from the boot, and returned to the front door. Elliot's eyes arrowed to Trixie.

'A dog,' he said.

Again, it was said as a statement, and I felt an irrational desire to yell at him. *Yes! Of course, it's a dog! What did you think it was? A pig?* I must have been more wound-up than I realised. I held my temper in check and nodded.

'This is Trixie,' I said. 'She's very friendly.'

'Mister Carlyle did not mention a dog.'

'I'm sure he won't mind. Can you take me to my room?'

Elliot hesitated for another second before nodding. He pointed me inside and passed through a stone entryway.

Beyond this lay a hall and a vast staircase ahead that divided into two directions as it reached an upstairs landing and a high window beyond. Both stairs led to the floor above. Glancing to my right, I spotted the biggest dining room I'd ever seen. I'd lived in apartments that were smaller. Off to my right was a hallway leading to what looked like a kitchen at the end. I glimpsed a woman down there, presumably a cook. She stopped at the entrance, glared at me, and shuffled out of sight.

'The ground floor east wing,' Elliot said, nodding, 'contains the dining room, library, billiard room, and parlour.' He pointed in the other direction. 'Servant's quarters and facilities are in the west wing.'

'Are there many...staff?' I asked, unable to say the word *servants*. It sounded too oppressive and Victorian.

'Just Lydia and I. She is both the cook and the maid.' He hesitated. 'Doctor Allen Shipley is also a frequent visitor. He's Mister Carlyle's personal physician.'

'Is that because of Alex Carlyle's health?'

'I will show you to your room.'

With this, he turned and started up the stairs.

Well, I thought. *That's one way to kill a conversation.*

6

I trailed up the stairs after him to the upper level where central corridors ran down the middle of the first-floor east wing. An imposing wall with a solitary door closed off the opposite side of the building. *Maybe that's Alex Carlyle's domain.* Lined up along the wall at eye level were several dozen photos. I guessed these were family pictures, although I couldn't be sure from here.

At least the interior of the building was warmer than the exterior. There was little sign of stonework. Almost everything was timber clad, making the place seem more like a manor house than a castle.

'How many bedrooms does the castle have?' I asked.

'Twelve.'

Wow, I thought. *This guy is really a chatterbox.*

'But you're not expecting that many this weekend?' I guessed.

'Mister Carlyle's family is attending, as is Doctor Shipley.'

He led me to a room at the end of the hall and pushed open the door, revealing a well-appointed chamber with an ensuite bathroom. There was a faint smell of dust which Elliot may have noticed too, judging by the way he was curling his nose. 'It's rare to have the whole family in residence.'

Maybe just as rare to clean, I thought, although possibly a little uncharitably. A building of this size was far too big for two people to upkeep. Surely something this big required a dozen staff? Alex Carlyle was made of money. Why didn't he hire more people?

Because he's stingy, of course. Alex Carlyle was renowned for being as tight as a drum. Which made it all the stranger that he was donating ten million dollars to our local hospital.

'And the family are?' I prompted.

He looked like he didn't want to answer. 'Simon Carlyle and his wife, Jasmine. Another son, Lachlan Carlyle, and Mister Carlyle's only daughter, Rani Carlyle.'

That tallied with what I already knew.

'Am I the first?'

As if in reply, raised voices came from behind the door of a room further down the hall. An argument.

'Both Simon Carlyle and his wife have arrived.' Although he managed to remain emotionless, it was only through the greatest effort. 'The other guests are arriving later.'

Trixie whined, and I patted her head. She didn't like arguments.

'I see,' I said. 'And Alex's bedroom...'

'Mister Carlyle's quarters are located in the west wing.'

So that was what lay beyond that single door on the other side of the stairs.

'There is one further matter of which you should be aware,' Elliot said. 'It concerns phone and wireless communication. Mister Carlyle has a standing rule regarding electronic devices. He dislikes them intensely and requests that people surrender their phones and any other devices while they're here.'

'You're kidding,' I said.

'I do not...kid.'

'So what if there's an emergency?'

'There is a landline downstairs.'

Wow, I thought. *A landline. That's the most ancient thing about the whole place.*

Elliot held out his hand, and I realised he wanted my phone. I felt like arguing, but what was the point? If I didn't comply, it meant I couldn't stay, and if I didn't stay, then the hospital missed out on a ten million dollar donation. After getting the landline number from him, I sent it to Kim, Nan, and Harry before reluctantly handing over my phone.

'And computer devices?' Elliot said.

Biting back an objection, I retrieved my laptop from my bag and handed it over.

'Dinner is at seven, followed by refreshments,' the butler continued. 'Do not be late. Mister Carlyle takes a dim view of tardiness.'

I took a dim view of a lot of things.

One of them was having my phone and internet access taken away. Elliot turned and left me standing in the room with my bag and Trixie. I silently closed the door, shutting out the sound of Simon and Jasmine's argument.

'No internet,' I complained to Trixie. 'We really are in the middle ages.'

After unpacking, I checked the room, and it was quickly evident that there wasn't a whole lot to see. My first impression that it could have been a hotel room in any town was correct. The light fittings were modern. So was the furniture.

Actually, it was more nineteen seventies drab than medieval: an outdated dresser with a big mirror, a rather uncomfortable bed, and timber wardrobes that wouldn't have looked out of place at trash and treasure.

A knock came at my door.

'Wonder who that is,' I murmured to Trixie.

Opening the door revealed a dour-looking woman with short greying black hair and narrow eyes. It was the woman I'd spotted in the kitchen. She stared at me without smiling.

'Miss Ryan?' she said.

'Rosie.'

'I'm Lydia Culp, Mister Carlyle's maid. He asked that I give you a tour of the building and grounds.'

'Is it possible for me to see him?'

'Later.'

Oh great. Another chatty employee, I thought. *Working for Alex Carlyle must be a barrel of fun.*

'Great.' I tried to sound cheerful. 'Let's go.'

I followed Lydia to the far end of the hall. The view from the window at the end was spectacular. I hadn't been aware of it on my drive, but the landscape had been gently rising. From here, I could just catch a glimpse of the distant ocean.

Peering down into the moat, I saw a trough of murky brown water. One side jutted up against the stonework of the castle. The other side met the lawn. Beyond this lay the short stretch of field, the pine tree forest, and the rolling landscape.

'It's quite a place,' I said.

'A big estate.'

Although lots of pine forests in Victoria were planted to harvest timber, that obviously wasn't the case here. 'Alex doesn't do anything with the forest?' I asked.

'Mister Carlyle has achieved everything he wants in life. A man like him deserves to rest at the end of his long journey and gaze out over his empire.'

Empire...?

This woman really needed to visit the outside world. She and

Elliot were quite a matching pair, and I wondered if they were a couple. It was hard to say. She seemed utterly sexless, and so did he.

'Have you worked for Mister Carlyle for long?' I asked.

'Forty years.'

'Goodness! That's a lifetime.'

She nodded without speaking and started back down the hall. We passed the door, where the argument continued. This was no minor spat. It was an all-out brawl, by the sound of it. Lydia made no indication that she noticed the raised voices. We reached the stairwell landing, and this time I looked more closely at the photos on the walls.

Before, I'd assumed that they were family pictures. I was wrong. On the left-hand side of the door were photographs of Alex and his business relationships. I glanced across the sea of images. There was Alex with a former Prime Minister. A photo of him with a media mogul. A picture of him shaking hands with a State Premier.

My eyes focused on a picture of him standing behind a shop counter, flanked by a group of workers. The sign in the background read *Carlyle Groceries: Open Till Late*. I nodded to the picture.

'This is Alex at his place of work?' I said.

'Just after the development of the Wishart inventory system. Those men helped him develop it. The company did very well after that.'

That was an understatement. From what I'd read, the company had gone from being worth a few million dollars to hundreds of millions in a few years. The Wishart system had rapidly become one of the world's leading shop inventory and reorder systems.

My eyes shifted to the photos on the other side of the door, and I frowned. 'What's this?' I asked.

Lydia stared at the pictures without emotion.

'Mister Carlyle loves his practical jokes,' she said. 'He says everyone must be able to take a joke. It's the measure of a man.'

In one photo, a man entering a room had a bucket of white goo splash down on his head. Another picture showed a woman sliding on a slippery floor. The third image was of a man terrified by a kangaroo in his office. I studied each of the images. There were dozens of them, and each showed people in embarrassing situations.

I looked closer. *Good grief.* One of the images showed Elliot sliding backward down the stairs. Another was Lydia finding what appeared to be a dead rat as she lifted a spoonful of soup from a pot. The poor woman looked horrified. It seemed no one was impervious to Alex Carlyle's practical jokes—if they could even be called that. There was a fine line between a practical joke and blatant sadism. It looked like Alex had no qualms about crossing that line.

I thought back to the glitter bomb and crushed red Jeep Wrangler I'd received in the mail. At the time, I'd thought it nasty. Compared to other people, it looked like I'd gotten off easy.

My stomach shifted uneasily. I hoped one of his nasty practical jokes wasn't what Alex had in mind for me. Swallowing my anger, I recalled what Harry had said about the ten million dollar donation. Was it real? Did Alex Carlyle really want me to tell his story? Or was I simply here for amusement value? If it weren't for the prospect of the hospital donation, I would have stormed out of the place.

'No one's ever sued him for one of his practical jokes?' I asked.

Lydia gazed at me without expression. 'Sometimes things have not gone as planned,' she said. 'I'll show you the rest of the house.'

Lydia started down the stairs, and I trailed after in silence. The window formed part of the rear curtain wall of the castle. It overlooked a section of field and the forest beyond. At the bottom of the stairs, Lydia led me to the enormous dining room. As I'd noticed earlier, it was a vast chamber dominated by a dining table surrounded by chairs. A single painting hung on a wall at one end with another on the opposite wall.

'That's Alex,' I said, nodding to one painting. He was much younger and looked solid and confident. The painting at the other end was a woman. Blond-haired, strong-boned, and vaguely Scandinavian. Lucy Carlyle, I presumed. I remembered reading about her. She was quite a beauty. 'Was that his wife?'

'Lucy Carlyle. A beautiful woman. Much missed.'

'She died in a home invasion? A robbery?'

Lydia's gaze lingered on the painting. It was hard to know what she felt. 'Were you close?' I asked. 'If you've worked for Alex for so long—'

'Mister Carlyle will tell you everything you need to know about his wife. She is much missed.'

Lucy died decades ago. Mourning her death after all this time seemed morbid.

Good grief, I thought. *How can anyone live here?*

We continued into a thin hallway that ran past several rooms. The first was a library.

I couldn't help but be impressed. The room had floor-to-ceiling bookshelves, and the books were old. Primarily classics, though there appeared to be several on finance. Possibly Alex was a reader. Maybe in his later years, with his health failing, there wasn't much else to do.

The next room leading off the hall was a billiard room. The table in the middle was immense. The chamber had the same stale smell of dust and disuse. I began to wonder if Lydia did much in the way of cleaning. Although to be fair, the building was so immense it would be hard to keep on top of everything.

I'd noticed that an interconnecting doorway led in here from the library. Similarly, another connecting door led from the dining room to the library. Lydia announced that the next room was a reading room. It appeared to simply be another room with a lounge. The one beside this was a smoking room. Again, it looked unused.

Goodness. And one man lives here with his two servants. It's ridiculous.

I thought of my own tiny home with Nan and Trixie. It seemed far more homely and full of love.

The door at the far end of the hall led unexpectedly to the outside world: a narrow alley facing the garage. Again, the somewhat incongruous timber building jarred against the image of the castle. I wondered why Alex had built it. Why not make it from stone to continue the illusion of the castle?

'The garage was built later,' Lydia explained, seeming to read my thoughts. 'Mister Carlyle did not want the expense and trouble involved in constructing another stone structure.'

She took me through the courtyard to the front door.

Although it wasn't that late in the day, it was already surprisingly dark in the courtyard. The high curtain wall blocked the afternoon sunlight. We re-entered the building, and Lydia stopped, pointing toward the west wing.

'That's the kitchen and staff facilities,' she said.

Lydia didn't seem inclined to continue the tour, so she nodded and said there was a bell in my room if I needed anything. I had barely acknowledged this when she turned and stalked off toward the kitchen.

Trixie and I exchanged glances.

'Lovely woman,' I murmured.

She gave a tiny bark in agreement.

I wasn't sure what to do, so I decided to return to the library. It had looked a charming room, and I'd always felt at home in rooms full of books. I followed the hallway and found the library door half-open.

Just as I went to push on it, I realised voices were coming from the other side.

'—you've got to keep your end of the bargain,' one said.

'The sooner the old man dies,' the other voice replied, 'the better.'

7

Entering the room was like pausing a play in mid-action. There were two players in the tableau beyond. One was Elliot, the butler. He was the one who had mentioned the bargain. The other man was someone who I vaguely recognised. He was a thickset man, around fifty, with prominent cheekbones and a mop of chocolate brown hair flecked with grey.

There was no mistaking the guilt on their faces. I'd walked in on something—but what?

Elliot was the first to recover. 'Miss Ryan,' he said. 'Can I help you?'

'Not at all. I was just taking a look around.'

'You're the journalist,' the other man said, still looking stunned by my appearance. 'Rosie Ryan?'

I recognised him. This was the eldest son. 'And you're Simon Carlyle?' I said, stepping forward and offering a hand.

He shook my hand and forced a smile. 'Yes,' he said. 'Nice to meet you. So you've joined us for the weekend's pleasantries?'

He grimaced. 'Not that there'll be many of those. Not with the old man around. He's a tough old salt, in case you didn't know.'

The smell of alcohol came off Simon in waves. I'd come across a few heavy drinkers in my time. Simon had that red-faced complexion of someone who drank too much. At the same time, I was sure he could hold his alcohol: hardcore alcoholics often could.

'A hardnosed businessman,' I said diplomatically.

'That's one way of putting it.'

The tolling of a bell came from the front door. Elliot excused himself, leaving me and Simon alone. We regarded each other awkwardly.

'It must have been quite an upbringing,' I said. 'Growing up in the castle.'

'I didn't do a lot of growing up here. My father made a point of sending us off to private schools.' He smiled without humour. 'He said it was for our education. I suspect he simply didn't like children. Of course, we came back for holidays, but he was often away on business. That's one thing about my father. He's a workaholic. Seven days a week. Every day of the year.'

'But he's retired now?'

'Not at all. He's still hard at it. You know he sold the controlling interest in Carlyle Groceries several years ago? Dad still receives a percentage of earnings. These days he mostly plays the stock market. Does well out of it too. He always had a knack for recognising a bargain. And as you say, he has always been hardnosed. Some might say ruthless.' His face darkened. 'Some might even call him a monster.'

As I struggled to think of something to say, the door swung open, and a woman appeared. She looked maybe ten years younger and had the same colour hair as the man, although it was crimped to the max. Her eyes zigzagged between Simon and me.

'Dear brother!' she said dramatically. 'And a strange woman I've never met! And a cute dog!' She embraced her brother briefly, firing air kisses at him before turning to me. 'I'm Rani. Simon's younger sister and far too attractive to be a Carlyle.'

I introduced myself and Trixie.

'Ah,' she said. 'The famous Rosie Ryan. And your canine pal. Rosie, I've heard you're quite an investigative journalist.'

'There's not a lot of investigative journalism to be done in Cape Carson. Mostly dog shows and local festivals.'

'You're too modest. I understand you were involved in tracking down a killer a while back.'

I didn't want to get into a conversation about the help I'd given the police. Truth be told, there had been more than one killer, but who was counting?

'Everyone's got a hobby,' I said. 'Mine's murder.'

She laughed too loudly, and I got the impression she did that a lot. I wondered what the real Rani Carlyle was like.

She turned to her brother. 'Have you seen darling Daddy yet?' she asked.

'He hasn't emerged from his inner sanctum. Probably still communing with Satan.' 'Don't be like that!' Rani swatted him. 'He's our beloved father.'

'If you say so.'

'And you'll give Rosie the wrong idea.'

Simon turned to me. 'You'll have to excuse me, Rosie,' he said. 'Our father has made it his mission in life to torment us.'

Rani shot him a look before turning to me. 'Daddy has a strange sense of humour,' she said. 'He likes to see if we can take a joke.'

'Depends how you define a joke,' Simon said. 'Some call it humour. Others might call it torture.'

'Simon,' Rani said in a warning tone.

He continued unconcerned. 'Growing up in the Carlyle house helps you to develop a thick skin,' he advised me. 'You had best watch out, Rosie. Father likes nothing more than to try his little...jokes on newcomers.'

I forced a smile. 'A whoopee cushion or similar?'

'That's entirely too tame. Who knows what clever little trick he has planned?'

The door opened, and another woman emerged. She was

tall, grey-eyed, and hailed from somewhere in Asia. Indonesia, possibly.

The only blemish in her appearance was a scar under her left eye. She greeted Rani warmly before introducing herself as Simon's wife, Jasmine. I remembered the furious argument I'd heard coming from Simon and Jasmine's room. There was no sign that anything had occurred as she greeted me and gave Trixie a pat.

'What a beautiful dog,' she said. 'I love beagles.'

'They're easy to love,' I told her.

Jasmine turned to Simon. 'We haven't seen your father yet?' she asked.

'Not yet. You know he loves to make a grand entrance.'

His wife nodded and seemed ready to continue when the door opened again. The newcomer introduced himself as Allen Shipley.

'You're Alex's doctor?' I said.

'One and the same.'

He was a handsome man and more smartly dressed than Simon. Whereas Simon wore what could be nicely termed as crumpled casual, the doctor wore a black suit and white shirt.

Rani spoke. 'I didn't know you'd been invited,' she said to him. 'This is turning into quite a party.'

'I'm here most days,' Allen said. 'Your father likes me to monitor his health.'

'And how is it?' Rani's eyes were suddenly attentive. 'His health, I mean.'

'Good. For a man of his age.'

Simon laughed unpleasantly. 'Rani,' he said. 'You really did miss your vocation.'

'What do you mean?' she asked.

'Your attentiveness to our father. You actually sound as if you care.'

'I *do* care.' She looked furious. 'He's *Daddy,* for heaven's sake!'

Simon chortled. 'You wouldn't be here if it weren't for his message.'

His message?

Jasmine lowered her voice. 'Simon,' she said. 'Our guests don't want to hear our family business.'

'Guests? You mean the good doctor and our journalist friend? They know what father's like. Everyone knows the reputation of the famous Alex Carlyle.'

Allen inclined his head. 'I'd better be getting to my room,' he said, obviously deciding to ignore Simon's ranting. 'I still have to unpack.' He turned to me. 'Rosie?'

'I'll head up too.'

Although I was dying to know what the family was discussing, this wasn't the time to linger. It was none of my business. Families fought, and having Alex Carlyle as a father wouldn't be easy for anyone.

Still, I wondered what Simon had meant about the *message*. As it turned out, I didn't have long to wait. Halfway up the stairs with Allen Shipley, he turned to me as raised voices came from the library.

'I wondered how long it would take,' he said. 'Before world war three broke out.'

'What's happening?'

Allen lowered his voice. 'It's the will,' he said quietly. 'It's *always* the will. Alex announces every few months that he's changing his will. It's like playing Russian roulette. Who are the winners and losers this time, we wonder.'

'What do you mean?'

'Determining who's in favour is a moveable feast. Alex changes his mind all the time. Simon's currently set to inherit the lion's share of the estate. Rani's getting a small portion. Lachlan—who hasn't arrived yet—is the less-favoured child. He's getting nothing.'

I hated prying, but I couldn't stop myself. 'And now?'

'Who knows? Alex keeps them on tenterhooks. It's horrible, really. My guess is that Lachlan will rise to the top again. As for Rani and Simon, who knows? If I were placing bets, I'd say Rani will remain in second place with Simon last.'

'You make it sound like a horse race.'

Allen laughed. 'I suppose I do,' he said. 'It's just that I've seen this happen a dozen times over the years. Alex Carlyle isn't a pleasant man—and I've told him that to his face. You know he's a practical joker? That extends to these terrible games Alex plays with his children. He pits them against each other.'

'I suppose there's a lot of money involved?'

'A hundred million dollars, give or take a few. Can you imagine what that would be like? One day Alex will die, and one child will inherit everything, while the others inherit zilch.'

We reached the upstairs landing. A long *dddrrrrrring* came from downstairs.

'Goodness,' I said. 'That's the landline. I suppose Alex's rule about electronic devices doesn't apply to you.'

'Quite the contrary. No one this weekend will have internet or phone access. That's one reason why the family has already started arguing. They're suffering from nomophobia.'

'From—what?'

'Anxiety caused by not having a mobile phone.'

'Surely you've made that up!'

'Not at all. Modern society is so connected to technology that we feel bereft without that constant connection.'

Actually, it made sense. Technology could be an addiction. 'So we're cut off from the rest of the world,' I said. 'What about television?'

'There are no TVs in Carlyle Castle.'

'Why?'

'Alex is rather old-school. Landlines instead of mobiles. Newspapers instead of the internet.'

'You and I are the only non-family members this weekend?'

'That *is* unusual,' Allen admitted. 'Alex mentioned he wants you to write an article? Something about a donation to the hospital?'

I nodded.

'I'm sure that will be part of it.' Allen sighed. 'Just keep your wits about you. Alex will have something *extra* planned. He always does. And it probably won't be pleasant!'

8

'Good grief,' I muttered. 'I've only been here a few hours, and I'm already losing my mind.'

I was sitting on the bed in my room. This was probably the longest time in years that I didn't have my phone or an internet connection. To make matters worse, I didn't even have a book. I hadn't thought to bring one, and I hadn't borrowed one from the downstairs library when I had the chance.

Thank goodness I had Trixie. She climbed onto the bed. 'How are you faring, girl?' I asked, stroking her neck. 'Are you going crazy too?' Trixie laid her head on my lap. She looked exceedingly happy, which made me smile. 'You're not suffering from nomophobia. You're too sensible for that kind of silliness. It's only people that get addicted to technology.'

I wondered if the arguing downstairs had finished, so I went to my door and cracked it open. There was no one in the hall. Another door opened, and a man I didn't recognise peered out.

It had to be the younger son, Lachlan. He had the same angular cheeks and hair colour. Lachlan was slimmer than Simon, however, and better built. Whereas Simon was going to fat—probably because of alcohol and fine food—Lachlan looked suntanned and healthy.

'Hello,' he said. 'We haven't met yet. You must be Rosie Ryan.'

'I am.' We shook hands. His grip was firm and businesslike. 'And you're Lachlan?'

'The same. I suppose my family has already warned you about me?' There was a teasing glint in his eye. 'Telling tales out of school.'

'Sorry to burst your balloon,' I said, grinning, 'but your name hasn't come up.'

'They must be on their best behaviour,' Lachlan said. 'How strange. Could it be to do with our father's will? Could it be that Simon has fallen out of favour again? And one of us is now in his good books? It's hard to say.' His face hardened. 'It's like that book, *1984*. One week Oceania is at war with Eurasia and allied with Eastasia. The week after, Oceania is allied with Eurasia and at war with Eastasia. It's constantly changing. Uncertainty is a horrible way to torture people. Fill them with hope and then dash it. That's my father's way. He's made a hobby of it.'

Lachlan seemed a little more down-to-earth than his siblings. Whereas Simon was a seething mess of emotions, and Rani was as theatrical as any actress on the stage, Lachlan seemed to say what he thought.

'It doesn't sound like you care too much,' I said.

His eyes met mine. 'Mind you, it's a lot of money. I'm assuming you're not a multimillionaire masquerading as an intrepid reporter?'

'The words *millionaire* and *Rosie Ryan* are never mentioned in the same sentence.'

'Then think of it this way, Rosie. A carrot gets waved over your nose, and that carrot is unimaginable wealth. It's so much money that you can have virtually anything you want, whenever you want it. The carrot is lowered, and you think you have it—and then it's snatched away. It's lowered again—and taken away just as fast. It's sickening if you want to know the truth.' He shook his head. 'I'm past caring, or I like to think I am. It's a lot of money. A lot of temptation. I'm just sick of the game. That's all.'

This was a lot of information to share with a complete stranger. 'Are you usually this open with people?' I asked.

'I haven't told you anything you won't hear tonight. I'm just getting in first. The family gatherings are all fun and games. Father does his best to tear us down or pit us against each other.'

It all sounded ghastly. *I wish I weren't here.*

Then I remembered why I was here and felt a little sick.

Alex does this with his children all the time. Tempts them with money and then threatens to take it away. And that's exactly what Alex has done with me and the donation to the hospital. It was a bribe to get me here.

But why? Did he really hate me that much? All from a silly argument over a parking space? And when did it happen? Years ago?

Lachlan's eyes slid past me. Elliot had quietly appeared. He seemed to be able to move without making noise. Maybe it was a skill he learned at butler school.

'Miss Ryan,' he said. 'Mister Carlyle has requested your attendance.'

It took me a moment to translate this into Rosie-speak. 'Alex Carlyle wants to see me?' I said. 'Now?'

Elliot inclined his head. 'Yes, miss.'

I glanced at Lachlan, who gave a small shrug. 'Royalty has summonsed you,' he said. 'King Carlyle himself has requested your presence. It would be bad form to say no.'

'And if I did say no?'

'Not a good idea.' A flicker of pain filled Lachlan's eyes. 'It wouldn't go down well.'

Then I suppose I'd better get this show on the road.

Flashing a quick smile at him, I followed Elliot down the hall and across to the other side of the landing. The butler unlocked the door. We crossed through a tiny passage into a single vast room broadly divided into three areas. One was a four-poster bed with giant pillows and a bedside table. The bedding looked dishevelled, and I wondered how often it was changed.

The next section of the room was a combined library and office. Pages littered the untidy desk in the middle, with piles of newspapers lying everywhere. Running across the two walls were bookshelves at least ten feet in height. They were stuffed with volumes, and the only way to reach the upper shelves was on a ladder. Fortunately, one sat nearby, though I couldn't imagine that Alex would have scaled it for a long time. That duty would fall to either Lydia or Elliot.

Next was the massive fireplace before which the lounge chairs sat. This was a good six feet across, with the motif of a dragon across the top. The interior was filled with charred timbers, and an untidy pile of firewood sat nearby. This would have seen a lot of action during winter; there was no sign of any other heating in the room. Now, however, it was summer and a long time since the fireplace had been lit.

A single glance told me that Alex Carlyle was much diminished. He sat between the lounge chairs in a wheelchair with a blanket over his knees. He had lost a lot of weight since I'd met him on that one occasion. Most of his hair was gone, and what remained was thin and wispy. His body was terribly gaunt. He gripped the edges of his wheelchair with talon-like hands. His face was like a death mask, the skin thin and yellow. He looked sick.

Alex wore a dressing gown that was well past its use-by date. It was hard to believe I was looking at one of the wealthiest men in the state. He could have passed for someone living alone in a cheap bedsitter.

And yet...

It was his eyes that gave me pause. Yes, he looked sick, but his eyes were glistening. There was still life in them, and maybe where his body was failing him, his mind was still alert. Sharp. And cruel. I could tell that in a single glance. He was like an old bear that had reached the end of its life and taken refuge in its cave. Although its method of hunting has changed, it is still dangerous. Lethal, even.

'Sit down, woman,' Alex said, a surprisingly deep and powerful voice emanating from his tiny frame. 'I'm not going to live forever.'

Elliot took his leave, exiting silently as I wandered over to the lounge chairs and sat. 'And it's lovely seeing you too, Alex,' I said. 'Still trying to perfect your parking?'

He laughed, and it was something between a bark and a growl. 'Then you haven't forgotten,' he said. 'Good. Memory is our most valuable asset. It stops us from making the same mistakes twice. And I hate making mistakes. Mistakes cost money. And time.'

He positioned himself opposite. I noticed there was no offer of drinks or refreshments. Common courtesy was outside of Alex's realm of thinking. His gaze settled on me like a spider examining a fly.

'It's hard to believe you've had such astonishing success as an investigator,' he said. 'There doesn't seem to be anything special about you.'

I felt myself flush. 'I'm not an investigator. I just help the police.'

'Don't insult me by downplaying your talents. I know you've solved several murder mysteries. You've even discovered killers that have operated quietly in the dark like rats. Somehow you've tracked them down and brought them to justice.'

'All right,' I said evenly.

The old man looked away.

'I've surrounded myself with smart people my whole life. It's what made me successful. Stupid people make stupid mistakes whereas smart people think differently and act differently.' He stared at me. 'That's why I wanted you, Rosie. Because you think differently. You know how people tick. You can help me.'

I stared at him.

'Help you?' I said. 'What about the hospital?'

'The hospital will get their money,' he said, waving a hand

dismissively. 'I need your help.'

'With what?'

He drew a long breath. 'Someone's trying to kill me.'

9

Time seemed to stand still.

'Kill you?' I said, finally.

Who would want to do that?

Of course, that was a ridiculous question. Who would want to kill Alex Carlyle? Who *wouldn't* want to kill him? Apart from his ruthless dealing with business associates, there was his fraught relationship with his children. I'd known them for only a few hours, and it was apparent none of them cared much for their father.

'Has there been an attempt on your life?' I asked.

He nodded. 'A parcel arrived for me,' he said. 'The return address was an antique bookstore from where I buy many old books. I immediately knew something was wrong with it, however, as the weight was all wrong.'

'And what was in the parcel?'

'An Eastern Brown snake.'

'A—*what?*'

He nodded soberly. 'One of Australia's deadliest snakes,' he said. 'A considerate soul had put some food in for the creature. They wanted it to survive. Oh yes. They wanted it to fulfil its mission.'

I stared at him.

Australia had some of the deadliest snakes in the world. Although the Eastern Brown didn't kill many people, that was because there was a good supply of antivenom around the country, and medical staff was trained to deal with bites. An untreated bite could kill someone in minutes. Someone in Alex Carlyle's condition wouldn't even make it that long.

'What did you do?' I asked.

'Fortunately, I already suspected a trick.' He smiled wryly. 'I've pulled many a practical joke in my time. The weight of the box was unevenly distributed. I knew something was wrong. Mind you, I didn't suspect a snake. After opening the box, I saw the contents, tossed it away, and yelled for assistance. Elliot and Doctor Shipley came running. The doctor cornered the creature and killed it with a fire poker.' He nodded to the cracked leg of the coffee table. 'Although he did damage my father's chestnut table. Still, I forgive him for that. The situation called for swift action.'

'What did the police say?' Although I immediately knew the answer. 'Wait a minute. The police said nothing—because you didn't tell them.'

Alex laughed. 'As I say, Rosie, you're a smart woman. You're right. The police were not informed.'

'Why not?'

'Because they're dolts and idiots. Besides, I deal with things in my own way. Quietly and in-house. Calling in outsiders is a bad idea.'

I stared at him. 'Hang on,' I said, frowning. 'Who do you think is responsible for this? Who exactly do you think wants to kill you?' The answer came to me almost immediately. 'I see. One of your children. They stand to inherit and have the most to gain. Is this why you're changing your will?'

Alex laughed. 'I suppose my brats told you that,' he said. 'Yes, I'm changing my will. It's not the first time, and it won't be the last. But they're the obvious suspects.'

'So who stands to inherit at present?' I asked.

'Simon, mostly.'

'And after?'

The old man shrugged. 'We'll see,' he said. 'Life is changeable.'

'And apart from your children...'

'Lydia and Elliot. And Doctor Shipley. The amounts are small, and I happen to know that they're not in dire financial straits. Besides, I've known all three for years. If they wanted to kill me, they would have done it a long time ago.'

'Some people are patient.'

'True, but why now? Any of them could have killed me a hundred times over and made it look like an accident. One of my children is trying to murder me. I need you to tell me which one.'

I thought for a moment. 'Alex,' I said. 'We've never been friends, and I doubt we ever would be.'

'I don't know.' Alex Carlyle laughed cruelly. 'There's a tenacity about you that is endearing. Misguided but endearing. And I liked the way you stood up to me when we quibbled over that parking spot. Most people stand down. You didn't. That's a trait to be admired.'

He had a strange way of admiring people. I'd barely spoken to the man for ten minutes and found him difficult. Being one of his children must have been nearly impossible. No wonder they seemed maladjusted. But now wasn't the time to think about that.

'You need to speak to the police,' I said. 'Todd Parker is the new sergeant in Cape Carson. He's a good cop. You want smart people? He's smart. A city cop. And he has resources that I'll never have.'

'I want you.'

'Why?'

'Because you care.'

Now it was my turn to laugh. 'I care?'

'Not about me,' Alex conceded. 'Oh, I saw that flash of

anger in your face when we tussled over that parking spot. For one brief second—one very brief moment—you would have liked to see me dead. That doesn't worry me. You know I mentioned your tenacity?'

'Endearing, but misguided?'

'You have morals. Believe in right and wrong. And you'll risk your life to discover the truth. To bring a criminal to justice. You're the person I need on my side.'

'And if I refuse?'

'Then you can leave.' He paused. 'But if you leave, there'll be no donation to the hospital. Not a cent. And that will be on your shoulders.'

I wanted to call him names my mother wouldn't have approved of. Instead, I clenched my jaw. 'This can't be an open-ended assignment. I have a life. I can't spend days, weeks, months—'

'A weekend,' Alex interrupted. 'That's all. Stay this weekend and watch the proceedings. I'll push people's buttons; I have a penchant for that. Watch my children's reactions. Observe. Give me your thoughts on which one wants me dead. That's all I ask.'

One weekend. A couple of days and this horrible ordeal would be over. The hospital would get its money, and I would have my freedom. And—maybe—I would have some idea of who wanted Alex dead.

'Let's assume I work out who hates you enough to want you dead,' I said. 'What will happen to the guilty party?'

'That's for me to determine. They are, after all, my own flesh and blood. I'm not an evil man. I don't kill people. The person responsible will be banished. That is all. They will cease to exist. They will have no call upon my fortune and will never be able to ask for my aid again.'

I didn't speak for a moment. What Alex did with his own family was his business. 'All right,' I said, finally. 'I can't make any promises. It is only one weekend, after all. But I'll do it.'

'Keep your eyes open,' Alex said firmly. 'I have a—if you like—a portent of doom. Something will happen this weekend. I don't know what. Watch my children. Keep alert.'

'I hope there's not an emergency. No one has mobile phones or internet access.'

'There's the landline downstairs.'

'Why the ban on technology?'

'The whole world is attached to those horrible things,' he said. 'Other than for business purposes, I've never spent a minute on them, and I'm glad. And, as I say, there's always the landline.'

'And if nothing happens?'

Alex smiled grimly. 'Then you'll see how the Carlyle family parties,' he said. 'We'll have a wonderful time.' The grin broadened. 'We always do.'

I got up to leave. Alex didn't speak until I'd almost reached the door.

'How is your grandmother?' he asked.

'Why do you ask?'

'We knew each other a long time ago.'

'Nan's fine. She's had a wonderful life.' I wanted to add without you but refrained. 'She mentioned you two used to date.'

'It was a long time ago, and it never would have worked. Still, it was good while it lasted.' He stared into space. 'And nothing lasts forever.'

10

The meeting with Alex Carlyle was over. He hit a button on his wheelchair, and Elliot appeared as if by magic. Soon, I was back in my bedroom and stroking Trixie's back as I watched the hands creep by on the clock. Everything the old man had said was passing through my mind like a whirlwind.

I wished I could speak to Kim, Todd, or Nan about it, but Alex's idiotic ban on mobile devices meant I was trapped in my own thoughts.

Someone's trying to kill me... One of my children is trying to murder me. I need you to tell me which one...

That's what he'd said. One of his children wanted him dead. The reason I was here—the real reason—was to give Alex my 'professional' opinion. Of Simon, Lachlan, and Rani, which one was most likely to carry out the deed?

Seven o'clock drew near. I did my makeup and fixed my hair before going downstairs. Here, I found Allen Shipley and the family standing about the dining room. Simon grasped a scotch glass in his hand. He and Jasmine were engaged in quiet conversation while Rani stood at the window and peered out at the darkening sky.

She turned and noticed me. 'Rosie!' she said. 'You're still here!'

'You didn't think I would be?'

'I had my doubts. If you're anything like the rest of us, you're going stark raving mad without your phone.'

'It's a bit of a challenge,' I admitted, turning to Allen. 'What about you, doctor?'

'To be honest, it's kind of a relief, although I did ring my practice to make sure everything was fine.' He nodded. 'It was. The partner I work with has everything under control.'

Rani turned to him. 'I forget you have patients other than Daddy.'

'Not many!' Allen said, laughing. 'Somehow, your father finds a way to take up most of my time.'

Both Simon and Jasmine's voices lifted above a murmur, and Simon said something about *budgets don't matter when you have money*. Jasmine shushed him, and I exchanged glances with Rani.

'Money problems,' she whispered. 'All is not well in Simon's household.'

I lowered my voice. 'Are they in business?' I asked. 'For themselves, I mean?'

'Real estate. But it's the age-old problem of having property you can't maintain. Although they own two blocks of units, both buildings are quite rundown and need extensive repairs. There's some major problem with the plumbing in one, and rising damp in the other. They can't repair the places because they don't have the money, and they can't get the money because they're so dilapidated. It's a catch twenty-two.'

'They can't sell them?'

Allen spoke up. 'They can, but they'd probably lose money. My practice isn't far from their buildings. I live in Briarbrook.' It was a small inland town. 'I know their properties. They really need work. Simon and Jasmine live in Briarbrook too, although in a rather more palatial part of town than me.'

'What about you?' I asked Rani. 'What do you do for a living?'

'I'm an influencer,' she said. 'Cosmetics.'

It was strange to think that a few short years ago, there was no such thing as an *influencer*. The word barely existed. Yet now, there were a whole host of people who promoted products and themselves, using social media to spread the word. Of course, there were some people who made lots of money from it and many who didn't.

'How's it going?' I asked.

'Absolutely fabulous,' Rani said.

Which is precisely what made me think she wasn't doing

well at all.

It wasn't that I'd never heard of her—I hadn't heard of most influencers—but she sounded slightly *too* enthusiastic.

The door eased open, and Lydia appeared with a tray of canapes. She sat them down and turned to leave.

'When's the old man coming down, Lydia?' Simon asked.

She slowly turned. 'I don't know,' she said. 'Mister Carlyle doesn't share his movements with me.'

Simon seemed ready to say something more but bit his tongue. He seemed to wither under her gaze.

After she left, Rani leaned close. 'Lydia has that effect on everyone,' she said. 'Lydia's always been rather like Mrs Danvers in *Rebecca*. She terrified us when we were kids, especially after our mother died. Mind you, Daddy packed us off to boarding school as soon as he could. He was never much for parenting.'

The door opened again, and Lachlan entered.

'Ah,' Simon said. 'Little brother has appeared. All will be set right with the world.'

'Simon,' Lachlan greeted him. 'Drunk already?'

'I'm never drunk. Just pleasantly inebriated.'

'Is that what it's called these days?'

'How's your little carpentry business?'

A flash of irritation crossed Lachlan's face before he forced a smile. 'Building,' he said. 'Building.'

With this, he poured himself a drink and joined us. Rani planted a kiss on his cheek. 'Ignore him, Lachlan,' she said. 'You know he's an idiot.'

'An alcoholic idiot,' Lachlan said. 'He's drinking himself to death and doesn't know it.'

'He probably does and couldn't care less. You know what Simon's like: you only live once.'

Lachlan sighed and turned to me. 'You must be sick of the Carlyle family already,' he said. 'Regretting that you accepted father's invitation?'

Actually, I'd regretted Alex's invitation until he told me the true purpose of my visit. Although I was no fan of Alex Carlyle, I had no desire to see him—or anyone—murdered. Now, mingling with his family, I was viewing them somewhat differently from how I'd seen them earlier.

One of them is a potential killer, I thought. *Which one?*

Alex could be wrong about Lydia, Elliot, and Allen Shipley. Maybe their financial positions were direr than he realised, and they needed a fast injection of cash. And then there was Jasmine. I had no idea what her thoughts were about Alex, although she may have seen his death as a cure for her and Simon's financial situation.

Or maybe none of these people intended Alex Carlyle harm. Anyone could have sent him that snake. An old business rival. Someone whom he'd wronged in the past. It could be anyone.

'I'm glad for the invitation,' I said diplomatically. 'It's nice to get away for the weekend.'

Simon spoke up. 'And Rosie's journeyed into the inner sanctum,' he said. 'And survived. Yes, Rosie, I saw you heading into father's lair. What did the old creature have to say?'

'You've already seen Daddy?' Rani looked insulted. 'He hasn't even seen me. Why did he want to speak to you?'

The room had collapsed to an abrupt silence, and all eyes were on me. I forced a smile. 'Alex is donating some money to Cape Carson hospital,' I said. 'I'm doing a story for the paper.'

Rani visibly calmed. 'A donation to the hospital?' she said. 'I'll believe it when I see it.'

'It's not the whole family fortune?' Simon asked, scoffing. 'Is it? I'm in favour of helping the underdog, but not if it means becoming one myself.'

I didn't answer this. 'Your father can speak for himself,' I said.

'I can indeed.'

Amid this last uncomfortable minute, the door had eased open, and Elliot had entered, wheeling Alex Carlyle. I had the distinct impression that the old man may have been listening for some time from the other side. His gaze shifted from one child to another.

'And I can do whatever I please with my money,' he said.

'Of course you can, Daddy,' Rani said. 'We wouldn't suggest

otherwise.'

'I can flush it all down the toilet if I want.' He wheeled himself to the head of the dinner table and told Elliot that Lydia could begin serving dinner. 'The rest of you—sit! You're hovering like vultures, and I'm not dead yet.'

We took seats, and I ended up positioned between Lachlan and Allen. Now that I took a closer look at the table, I saw it was professionally set, although the crockery was old and some pieces were chipped. Alex Carlyle was certainly frugal with his money. Our dining set at home was in better shape than this.

'How have you been, father?' Simon asked carefully.

'Alive. At my age, waking up is a combination of surprise and regret. The longer you live, the more you realise it's all more of the same.' He scanned the visitors. 'Although we're not all often together at the same time. It's nice for a man to see his loved ones assembled. Reminds him what his life has been about.'

Alex's eyes rested on me momentarily, and I could almost read his mind.

Watch and listen.

'Are you reading anything interesting?' Rani asked.

'Only the usual business periodicals. Business is easy once you make a lot of money. Mistakes are cushioned. Errors more easily rectified.'

'Oh yes,' Simon said, nodding enthusiastically. 'I know what you mean.'

Alex shot him a look and didn't reply.

The door opened. Lydia and Elliot silently entered and placed entrees before us: grilled chicken with cherry salsa. I inhaled. Goodness, maybe Lydia was like the dastardly Mrs Danvers from *Rebecca*, but she could certainly cook.

My delight in the food was broken by Alex's voice.

'Do you?' he snapped at Simon. 'What are you saying?'

Simon swallowed. 'Just that I know what you mean.'

'Explain yourself.'

'Well,' Simon began, reddening, 'it's easy to make mistakes in business. It's hard to fix them when you don't have the funds.'

Everyone had started eating. Even Alex. Although I tried not to watch, it was like watching a car crash in slow motion.

'So?' Alex continued, chewing slowly.

'I'm saying you need financial backing. Everyone knows that money makes money.' He seemed to shrink. 'Our properties need money to bring them up to scratch.'

'You're talking about those blocks of units? Those slums you invested in that I said should have been knocked down?'

'They made us good money for a while. And the value of the properties has gone up considerably—'

'Any idiot can make money from property!' Alex snapped. 'The housing market has been on the rise for decades. You needed to reinvest your earnings. Not squander it on speculative idiocies.'

People were behaving as if nothing was happening. Maybe this was par for the course at Alex's dinners. From everything I've heard, it probably was. While Simon floundered, I noticed his wife Jasmine had stopped eating. She held her knife and fork so hard that her knuckles had whitened.

'That company was highly recommended to us,' she said evenly.

'By your brother,' Alex said. 'I'm sure he was completely unbiased, despite being the company director.'

'I haven't heard about this,' Rani interjected. 'What kind of business is it?'

'It was a new social media firm,' Jasmine said, turning to her. 'It combined a platform for people to communicate using deep fake imagery. You could literally change your face to be anyone you wanted to be.'

'A sound idea,' Simon added.

'Except for the legalities.' Alex was eating his chicken like a dog chomping on dog food. 'It turns out people own their own faces. What a surprise. And billions of people on Earth didn't want their images used without their permission.'

'We didn't realise—'

'Any good lawyer would have told you,' Alex said, cutting him off. 'So it was a lot of money down the drain for no good reason. And you own that ridiculous boat too. What's it called? The *Voyager*? Have you never heard the old adage? Boats are holes in the water into which you throw money? Another costly mistake.'

Jasmine had paled. 'Yes,' she said tightly. 'Another costly mistake.'

She turned back to her food. I wasn't sure if she was trying to fight back tears or contain her rage. It could have been both.

'And my darling Rani,' Alex continued, either unaware or uncaring about his effect on the others, 'the *influencer*. Have you *influenced* many people of late, my dear?'

Rani's smile froze. 'My following is growing. Getting bigger by the day.'

'I understand you've just purchased several thousand of them from a dealer in Nigeria.'

'I...I don't know what—'

'You know exactly what I'm talking about. And there was that deal you made with that cosmetics firm. What a superb choice that was.'

Rani said nothing.

'Except those skin lotions were found to be toxic,' Alex went on. 'And the manufacturer is now being sued. Perhaps you should have investigated more before agreeing to that ridiculous contract.'

'Yes,' Rani said flatly. 'I suppose I should.'

'And the girl you lent that money to—'

Rani's face flared. 'How do you know about—'

'I know everything!' the old man snapped. 'I didn't get where I am by being stupid.' He turned to Lachlan. 'And talking about stupid...'

Unlike his siblings, Lachlan looked nonplussed. Even amused. 'I wondered when it would be my turn,' he said. 'I hate missing out on things.'

'How many businesses have you run into the ground?' Alex sneered.

'I'm sure you know, beloved father.'

'*Six*.' The word hung in the air. '*Six* failed enterprises that you started and killed with your ineptness. The fast food restaurant. The cleaning firm. The gardening service—'

'Don't bother listing them. I was there.'

'And I was there too! Bailing you out at every opportunity. And what are you now? A *carpenter*. A *tradesman*.'

'It's an honest job,' Lachlan said quietly, now meeting his father's gaze for the first time. 'Have you always been honest?'

'Honesty is for fools.'

Elliot removed plates as the main course arrived: steak and vegetables. Classic Australian cooking, and I didn't mind a bit. At least it proved a distraction from Alex's constant barbs. We ate in silence for a few minutes. At one point, Allen noticed me and raised an eyebrow as if to say *what do you think of all that?*

I gave a tiny nod and focused on my food.

What did I think of it? There was an old saying about the ability of power to corrupt, and that's what had happened to Alex. He had worked hard, as had his father, and his work had produced incredible results. But corruption killed as well. It had deadened him as a person. Made him bitter. Resentful. Solitary. Those feelings extended to how he felt about his own family.

Then there were his assets. How many families had been torn apart by siblings squabbling over money and possessions? The sums could be big or small.

Brothers and sisters had ended relationships over soup bowls and artwork and favourite furniture. I had cousins who no longer spoke to each other because of a sideboard. It had been promised to each of them and had gone to the one who reached the house first after the funeral.

Families, I thought. *There's no hatred like that experienced by one family member for another.*

No wonder Alex Carlyle was worried for his life.

11

Although dessert is usually my favourite part of any meal, there was none on this occasion, for which I was grateful. At the end of the meal, Alex signalled Elliot, who stepped forward to wheel him from the room.

'Good evening to you all,' Alex said. 'I'll see you in the morning.'

'Daddy,' Rani began hesitantly. 'May I inquire about your will?'

'What about it?'

'You're making some changes.' She glanced at the others. 'You told us that via your letter. Changing the will affects us all—'

'I am changing my will,' Alex confirmed, cutting her off. 'Rewriting it completely. I'm dissolving all my assets, turning everything into cash, and tossing it into the ocean.'

'But Daddy—'

'Or maybe that's one of my little jokes. You know how much

I love my practical jokes.'

Jasmine unconsciously rubbed the scar under her eye. Her jaw tightened.

What's that about? I wondered.

'Father—' Simon began.

'Goodnight.'

Elliot wheeled him from the room.

Silence settled over the table in his wake before Simon began swearing under his breath. Jasmine took his hand and squeezed it. Rani looked ill as Lachlan stared broodily into his glass of wine.

'I hate him,' Simon seethed. *'I wish he were dead!'*

Jasmine tightened the grip on his hand. 'Simon, don't—'

'I do! I wish he were dead!'

Rani gave a hollow laugh. 'Well, Simon,' she said. *'Everyone* wishes that. But wishes don't achieve anything.' She took a long breath. 'Maybe we can hire a hitman. Rosie, you know people. Do you know a hitman we can use? If we all chip in—'

'Don't even joke about it,' Lachlan said. 'He's our father.'

'Who's joking?' Rani said, all trace of humour gone from her face. 'That's our inheritance he's talking about tossing into the ocean.'

'Is he serious?' Simon asked, his face pale. 'God help us. If he's serious...'

'He's not serious,' Lachlan said. 'You know what father's

like.'

Simon turned to Allen. 'You know the old man, Allen,' he said. 'You're his doctor. Is he serious about throwing his money away?'

Allen shrugged. 'Your father says things...'

'But to just toss it away—' A thought struck Simon. 'It's *insane*. Only an *insane* person would do such a thing. Allen, if he's insane, then any will he makes is worthless. A judge would decide the inheritance. He *must* be declared insane. You can see that, Allen.'

The doctor looked uncomfortable. 'I'm not a psychiatrist,' he said. 'Only a general practitioner and I doubt a psychiatrist would find him insane.'

Simon slammed his fist on the table. '*But it's our money!*' he yelled. 'It's *our* money. He can't take that away—'

Lachlan glanced at his watch. 'Well,' he said. 'This has been delightful, but I'm off to bed.'

His brother gaped. '*Bed?*' he said. 'But we need to decide what to do about father.'

'I already know what I'm doing about father. Nothing. I'm going to bed and leaving in the morning. The old man might leave his money to us or feed it to the fish. I have no idea, and I'm not particularly concerned. I can't do anything about it, so I'm off to bed. I'll see you all in the morning.'

Without saying another word, he left, leaving a stunned

room in his wake.

'We…' Simon struggled for words. 'We need a plan—'

Rani stood. 'Simon, we can't lose any sleep over this. You know what Daddy's like. He has his little jokes. He loves them.' She swallowed. 'His *funny* little jokes…' Her voice trailed away as she glanced at Jasmine. '*You* know what his jokes are like. Talking about tossing his money into the sea is probably just another. We need to ignore him and get on with our lives.'

She left, and the remaining brother swigged down the last mouthful of his drink. 'Rani could be right,' he said. 'Or wrong. In the meantime, the only sensible thing to do is to get terribly drunk.'

'Darling—' Jasmine began.

'And why not? The old man has given us nothing. We may as well drink his booze and take what we can.' He clenched his fists. 'I was the main beneficiary of the will up till now. That's about a hundred million. Or I might be left with nothing. Once he changes his will—'

Allen stood. 'Best if I call it a night, too,' he said. 'Rosie? Are you heading upstairs?'

Actually, I wanted to hear Simon. It sounded like he practically wanted to race upstairs and throttle his father. Now Simon stared at me as if realising what he'd been saying.

'Rosie,' he said. 'You mustn't take our family squabbles too seriously. We're always like this. It'll be forgotten by morning.

Father's a practical joker. Did you know that?'

'Yes,' I said, standing. 'A practical joker.'

But there was nothing funny in anything I'd heard at dinner. It was more like a Shakespearean tragedy than a family dinner. Following Allen from the room, I went upstairs and lingered in the hallway leading to the bedrooms. Both Lachlan and Rani had already disappeared. Allen nodded to the door closest to the stairs.

'This is my room,' he said. 'I hope you have a good night's sleep, Rosie. Some might find it hard sleeping after that.'

I lowered my voice. 'I'm glad I'm not a member of the family.'

'I've had that thought myself.' He paused. 'Although, strangely, I rather like Alex sometimes. His brain is incredible. No doubt about that. He's a genius in his own way. And people carry on about his practical jokes. I've never been a victim, fortunately. I think money's ruined him. It's a shame. Money can do that sometimes.'

I nodded, wished him goodnight, and went to my room. Trixie greeted me enthusiastically. Settling onto the bed, I turned out the light and gave her tummy a good rub.

My goodness, I thought. *What an awful night.*

Resting my head back on the pillow, I peered into the dark night beyond my window. The sooner I got back to Cape Carson, the better. At the same time, my thoughts returned to what Alex had said.

Someone's trying to kill me.

Who could that be? There were so many of them. People were practically lining up. His children, business associates, people whose parking spaces he'd stolen. My eyes closed. If I just focused for a moment...

I awoke with a start. Gosh, I must have been more tired than I'd realised. It was two o'clock, and I'd fallen asleep fully clothed.

A flash of light burst through the window. Lightning! A rumble of thunder followed almost immediately. A summer storm had rolled in during the night. Rain fell gently against the bedroom window.

Trixie was asleep.

I eased her off the bed and got into my pyjamas. Nan had bought me a nice pair decorated with flamingos. After settling myself comfortably, I was drifting off to sleep when I heard a sound from the hallway. *Go to sleep*, I thought wearily, and then my journalistic instinct cut in. Groaning, I climbed out of bed and crossed to the door. Easing it open, I peered out. The hallway lay in darkness, with only the tiny sconces attached to the walls providing soft illumination.

A figure turned the corner of the stairs and headed down.

Who is that?

I followed quietly, padding after them in the dark. Reaching the top of the stairs, I was in time to see them disappearing down the east wing hallway. I still couldn't make out who it was. Racing down, I crept to the edge of the wall and peered down the darkened passageway. The far door leading out to the garage eased open, revealing a deeper darkness, and the person disappeared through.

Creeping after them, I gazed out the window into the gloomy alley beyond. A light rain fell into the gap between the buildings. There was no movement. Nothing. Then the tiny light of a torch flickered on in the garage. The cool air of the night chilled me as I went outside. I shivered, stifling the urge to sneeze. Taking care to move slowly, I went to the door leading into the garage and took refuge under the awning. At least I was dry under here.

The door was open a crack. Scrutinising the interior, I glimpsed a figure in the gloom.

Jasmine.

A muffled voice spoke.

'That may be true,' Jasmine said. 'But we can't keep going like this forever!'

The two continued speaking for a moment until Jasmine laughed. 'Maybe,' she said. 'Accidents happen—especially at sea!'

I eased the door open another inch—and it creaked like a coffin opening in a horror film! Jasmine uttered a small cry, and

I turned tail and fled back into the house. Hurrying down the corridor, I glimpsed a lighted figure coming down the stairs ahead, so I blindly pushed open the nearest door and took refuge.

It took a moment for my eyes to grow accustomed to the gloom. *I'm in the billiard room.* I'd only seen this briefly. *I should be safe.* I waited a few seconds as I listened to approaching footsteps—and then they receded into the distance.

Thank goodness!

Lightning flashed again, followed by an even louder peel of thunder. The rain began bucketing down.

It's a raging storm out there!

I leaned into the hall and saw Jasmine disappearing up the stairs. As I went to leave, I heard the murmur of voices from nearby. They must be from the person I'd briefly glimpsed descending the stairs.

Where are they?

The library was next door.

Why would someone be in there at this time? *It's a bit late for reading!* Creeping to the connecting door, I placed my ear against it. I was right. A voice came from the other side. I gripped the door handle and eased it open an inch.

'...only a matter of time.'

Rani!

What was she doing here in the middle of the night? And her

manner of speech was downright furtive. *Who is she speaking to?* I angled my body slightly. A faint light filled the room, but I could only see her elbow.

Although I didn't hear an accompanying voice, she was clearly listening to someone because she spoke again after a brief interval.

'...it isn't easy, especially when it's someone you've cared about.'

What?

She seemed to listen for an interminable time before saying she had to go. That was my signal too. I didn't want to get caught here, especially after what I'd just heard. Gently closing the door after me, I didn't risk staying where I was, so I crept away from the door and hid under the billiard table.

Good grief, I thought. *What have I just heard?*

Was Rani plotting her father's murder? If so, who was she speaking to? I wasn't able to see the other person. It couldn't be Jasmine. She had returned upstairs. Who else could it be?

After waiting another ten minutes, I rose from my hiding place and opened the door to the hallway. Empty. The whole household was finally asleep.

About time!

It sounded like the rain was subsiding too. I made my way along the corridor to the bottom of the stairs and was about to ascend when I heard more voices. *You've got to be kidding!*

Does no one sleep around here? I glanced at my watch. It was after two-thirty now. Who was up and about at this time? The voices were coming from the west wing of the building.

I hesitated. I was exhausted, yet this was an opportunity to learn more, and I'd be a fool to pass it up. I crept towards the kitchen. Lightning flashed, giving me a glimpse of what lay ahead.

The voices grew louder. At least this time, I could hear—and recognise—both speakers. One was the dour Lydia Culp, and the other was Allen Shipley. A band of light shone from under the kitchen door. I crept closer until I could understand what was being said.

'...haven't got long anyway,' Lydia was saying. 'Surely there's another way?'

'It's necessary.'

'But the end is coming soon.'

'I know. Though it doesn't mean—'

An enormous crash came from the other end of the build-ing. I bit back a gasp and stepped back in fright as the racket was immediately followed by a yell. It sounded as if someone had fallen down the stairs. I raced in that direction and found a groaning form at the bottom.

'Hello?' I said as I tried to identify the person. 'Are you all right?'

Then a lot of things happened at once. A light came on in

the landing above, and Jasmine appeared. At the same time, Allen and Lydia came up behind me as Elliot appeared from another west wing corridor.

The butler was momentarily unrecognisable. He wore a dressing gown and pyjamas. Out of his formal attire, he could have been anyone.

I gazed at the groaning form at my feet.

'Simon?' Jasmine called. 'My God! Are you all right?'

Her husband rolled over. 'Took a tumble,' he muttered. 'One of those steps must be faulty. Got to get that fixed...'

The stench of alcohol coming off him would have put a brewery to shame. Allen knelt down and told him not to move. The doctor's eyes met mine.

'I came down to get a glass of water,' I said. 'I didn't know Simon was behind me, or I would have offered to help.'

Lydia's eyes bored into me. 'There's a glass in your room,' she said.

'Trixie was naughty and drank out of it earlier,' I fibbed. 'She usually doesn't do that. Must be worried, being away from home.'

By now, Allen had examined Simon, and the man was waving him away. 'I'm fine, Allen,' he said, staggering to his feet. 'I bounce. It's one of my many talents.'

I peered up the stairs and took in the sea of faces.

Jasmine had already started down. Lachlan was leaning over

the balcony railing with Rani beside him. The only person not here was Alex Carlyle, who was clearly still asleep.

'You're lucky you didn't hurt yourself,' I said to Simon. 'Why were you wandering about in the middle of the night?'

'Felt like a walk.'

'At two-thirty in the morning?'

'Good for my constitution.'

I clearly wasn't about to get a sensible answer from him.

Jasmine grabbed his arm and helped him up the stairs. I glanced back at Lydia, who was watching me carefully. I gave her a brief nod and followed the others up the stairs. When I glanced back down again, the old lady was still there, her eyes fixed on me.

Returning to my room, I went inside to find Trixie still sound asleep on the floor. The storm had passed. Thunder rolled, but it was miles away. I climbed into bed and lay in the dark.

What a weird night, I thought. *At least tomorrow can't be as strange as today.*

How wrong I was.

12

Sunlight streamed into the dining room.

The storm from the previous night had passed, heralding another bright and glorious summer's day. It seemed to make the group gathered around the table appear all the more shattered. Simon was the worst. Despite being a heavy drinker, the previous day had clearly taken its toll. Deep rings hung under his eyes, and his face was blotchy. Lachlan had finished early. So had Rani, but they both looked exhausted. The only people who seemed vaguely refreshed were Jasmine and Allen. Even Lydia looked a little unsteady on her feet as she carried in breakfast on a tray.

We had two cereals to select from for breakfast, and both looked cheap and nasty. If this were a hotel, they'd be out of business in a week. I poured some dry cereal into a bowl and splashed milk on top.

I can hardly wait to get out of here, I thought. *When will this weekend be over?*

A knocking came from somewhere within the house. No one reacted at first. Then Allen glanced up sharply. Without speaking, he rose and crossed to the door.

'Hope everything's okay,' I said.

'I'm sure it is,' Allen said.

He didn't sound sure. I followed him out and up the stairs. Elliot was hammering hard on the door leading into Alex's domain. The butler turned at the sound of our steps.

'Mister Carlyle's not answering,' he said.

'And he usually does?' I said.

'Every morning.'

Allen knocked at the door and continued for several seconds as a herd of people clattered up the stairs. Everyone spoke at once—which resulted in minimal action—until Lachlan raised his voice and said the door had to be broken down.

It was easier said than done. Allen tried. Then Lachlan joined him, the door finally shattered, and the lock went flying. We piled into the room after them. There was a collective registration of utter shock—and then Lydia screamed.

Alex Carlyle was dead. A rope had been tied around his body, and a gag placed around his mouth. A knife had been jammed to the hilt into his left eye socket. I gazed in utter shock at the motionless form. It was so horrifying that I could not think. Then a single thought ran through my mind.

Someone's trying to kill me.

The old man had said it himself.

And now it had come true. I turned away from the gruesome sight to see Rani shaking. 'Get an ambulance,' she shrieked. 'We need an ambulance.'

Allen quickly checked the old man's body.

'It's too late for that,' Allen said. 'He's dead. Killed instantly, I'd say.'

Simon sagged against his wife and made inarticulate sounds. He was unsuccessfully trying to form words. 'Suicide,' he said. 'That's...that's the only explanation...it can't be...'

'Don't be ridiculous!' Lachlan snapped angrily. 'He's been murdered.'

'Everyone out,' Allen ordered. 'This is a crime scene, and we need to call the police.'

We turned away from the horrible sight. As one group, we staggered back out the door.

'We need our phones,' Jasmine said. She seemed in better shape than the three siblings. 'Where are our phones? Elliot?'

The butler was pale. 'I...I don't know. Mister Carlyle never told me. He always hid them when I wasn't around.'

'There's a landline downstairs,' Allen said.

Like an unruly herd of sheep, we staggered to the stairs and started down. I couldn't get the image of the dead man from my mind. It was like something from a horror film. We had just reached the landing when Jasmine gripped the window sill for support—and gave a small cry.

'Look!' she yelled. 'There! A man's running into the forest!'

Allen joined her. 'I see him!' he said. 'No! He's gone now.'

'It must be the killer!'

'Quickly!' Lachlan yelled. 'We've got to ring the police!'

Our ramshackle group tore down the stairs in pursuit. Elliot snatched up the landline phone—and then hammered the plunger several times. He stared down in confusion at the lead running to the wall. Allen snatched it up.

'This has been cut,' he said. 'The line's dead.'

Simon cursed. 'The killer's getting away!' he said. 'We've got to catch him. Come on, everyone! Quickly!'

We raced out of the castle, across the bridge, and into the field. Lachlan pointed to where they'd spotted the stranger, and we tore into the woods.

'Spread out!' Allen called. 'Yell if you see him!'

I wasn't sure that was such a good idea.

The killer had already struck once; a second murder wouldn't bother him at all. But I couldn't argue with them. People were already spreading out in a long cordon.

Trixie barked. I was glad I had her beside me. At least she could provide some kind of protection. I staggered through the woods, catching scattered glimpses of the others. First, there was Lachlan, and then I lost sight of him and spotted Jasmine. Then Elliot. Lydia. Everything became a confused smattering of trees and figures hurrying through gaps in the woods like a stop-motion film.

I was out of shape and puffing badly. By now, I'd completely lost track of everyone else. My run slowed to a stagger. *This is crazy. We should have stayed together.* For all we knew, the killer could have taken refuge and doubled back. He could be lying in wait to kill someone else. We were scrambling about like mice in a maze.

A grey shape loomed ahead: a road. I pushed my way through some underlying growth. This road bordered the huge estate. A sense of unease gripped me. If I encountered the killer alone...

A bedraggled figure emerged from a grove of trees further down the road. 'Rosie?' Simon said, swatting away leaves and branches. The man looked a mess. 'Did you see him? The killer?'

I shook my head. 'What about you?'

'Only for a few seconds. I tried to catch him, but I'm too out of shape.'

I peered up and down the road. This would have provided the perfect getaway. He had his car waiting. After committing the murder, the killer hoped to escape without being seen. Fortunately, Jasmine and Lachlan had glimpsed him at the last moment.

Simon yelled out, and Rani appeared from the trees. The

three of us returned to the house to find Allen waiting. He told us that Elliot and Lydia had taken her car and driven to a neighbour's house to fetch the police. The remaining members of the group—Jasmine and Lachlan—staggered back to the house.

Everyone seemed in a state of shock. We reassembled in the dining room, where I poured cold tea and coffee for the group. Only Allen seemed in possession of his senses. He asked that no one leave the room; the police would want to search the house for clues.

By the time Lydia and Elliot returned, the sound of sirens filled the air. Todd Parker and Constable Jim Turner went to Alex's room while the rest of us were asked to wait in the library.

I slumped into a chair. It wasn't midday yet, and I already felt exhausted. So much had happened in the last few hours. Trixie licked my hand, and I absently patted her head.

Someone's trying to kill me.

Alex Carlyle had called it a premonition, and he'd been proved right. While I didn't usually believe in such things, there was no doubt that his intuition had proved correct. After a few minutes, Todd joined us in the library, and he asked me to step outside for a moment. I expected him to berate me for being at the scene of yet another murder. Instead, he was surprisingly supportive.

'This must be a horrible shock,' he said.

My thoughts returned to my glimpse of the dead man: his bound body, gagged, the knife in his eye.

'I'm okay,' I said. 'Although it is terrible: the stuff of nightmares.'

'I don't suppose you can leave the investigating to me?'

My eyes met his. 'Have you ever known me to interfere?'

'Is that a rhetorical question, or are you serious?'

I glared. 'I'm only being helpful,' I said.

'And I suppose you'll be ringing Kim the moment my back is turned. You'll ask her to join you and begin interviewing everyone the first chance you get?'

'I am a journalist,' I reminded him. 'It is my job.'

Todd sighed. 'Then all I'll ask is that you keep me in the loop.'

'I can do that.'

'All right,' he said, reluctantly reaching into his pocket. 'We found everyone's phones. They were in a drawer in Alex's room.'

I gripped my phone like meeting an old friend. Todd asked me for a rundown of everything I'd seen. He took notes, only interrupting with the occasional question. At the end, Todd gave me a quizzical look. 'Alex Carlyle knew someone wanted to kill him?' he said.

'Someone even made an attempt with that snake.'

'And he didn't contact the police?'

'No offence, but he didn't have faith in the police. Barely had faith in anyone, as far as I can make out.' I paused. 'Do you know much about him?'

'Hardly anything.'

I told Todd about my parking encounter with Alex Carlyle and some of his past history. 'He was a horrible piece of work,' I said thoughtfully. 'I think his constant striving for success warped him.' I shook my head. 'Shame you missed the dinner last night. He gave his family a real serve.'

'But not you?'

'Or Lydia or Elliot or Allen.'

Todd sighed. 'Well,' he said. 'I suppose I'll launch into the breach. Try not to get in my way. Or carry out any break and enters. Or put your life in danger.'

'I'm ringing Kim,' I said, pouting.

Todd groaned. 'Then we're all in serious trouble.'

'Can I ask you a question?' I asked, ignoring him.

'I think you just did.'

'Do you know how the killer escaped? The first we knew was when Jasmine spotted him from the stairwell window.'

Todd nodded. 'There are servants' stairs leading from Alex's room,' he said. 'They angle down around the back of the building. A window was open about halfway down. It seems the killer jumped from the window into the moat and swam to the other side. There are scuff marks on the other side of the moat. From there, he raced across the field into the forest.'

'He's lucky the jump into the moat didn't kill him.'

'The moat's surprisingly deep. It's only gets shallow when you reach the other side.'

I nodded. 'So Elliot would have had access to the stairs?'

'The butler? Sure. And the maid. Except both have already told me those stairs haven't been used in years.'

Todd promised he'd keep me posted and disappeared into the library. I took the opportunity to escape to the courtyard with my phone. I gave it a brief pat. *My precious*, I soothed, feeling more than a little like Gollum from Lord of the Rings. *I've got you back! You're mine forever!*

13

I rang Kim and gave her a brief rundown.

'Good grief!' she said. 'Of course, I'll help. You know I love a good murder.'

'Yes,' I agreed. 'Although it's always better when it's someone else.'

'Absolutely. Being on the receiving end is a real downer.'

She promised to join me within the hour and, true to her word, was soon pulling up outside the castle. I met her in the courtyard, where she gave me a huge hug.

'You're still a bit shattered,' she said.

'I am,' I admitted. 'Every time I close my eyes I think of Alex Carlyle's dead body.'

'Talking about eyes...'

'Yes, a knife to the left eye is a pretty gruesome way to die.'

She shuddered. 'It's horrible.' Kim lowered her voice. 'So Alex Carlyle wanted you here because his life was in danger?'

'A squad of armed guards would have been a better idea,' I

said. 'He might still be alive today.'

'And there's no suspects?'

'Not yet. Alex was worried about one of his children wanting him dead.'

'What do you think?'

'The killer seems to be an outsider, but he may have had inside help. Someone could have let him into the castle.'

'Maybe we should start with the staff.'

'Lydia idolised him. I can't think why. She seemed to think he was some kind of great man.'

We went back inside and found the woman preparing food in the kitchen. I hadn't seen this area before. It was a full commercial kitchen with brat pans and a huge oven with bake and steam controls. Likewise, the dishwasher was huge.

You could produce food for a hundred people, I thought. *It's complete overkill for a man living in isolation.*

The woman looked up from the bench where she was dicing carrots. I had no idea who she was cooking for, although she must have felt that *the show must go on*. Or maybe she was trying to stay busy.

'Lydia,' I said. 'I wanted to see how you're coping.'

The woman looked up at me with her dark eyes, and I had the impression that she was barely concealing her rage. 'How do you think I'm coping?' she asked. 'Alex Carlyle was the most incredible person I've ever known. He built an empire and provided employment for thousands. Mister Carlyle should have been allowed to die quietly in his sleep. Instead—' She clenched her hands tightly. 'He must be avenged.'

I stared at her. Judging by her reaction, it would have been easy to believe that another murder was about to happen at any moment. For the first time, she seemed to notice Kim at my elbow. Once the introductions were completed, I asked Lydia how long she'd known Alex.

'Years. Almost forty years. From the time his business really started to take off. Back in those days, it was still a small chain of stores. Over time it grew.'

'And you've always been his...' Kim hesitated over the word '...maid?'

She shook her head. 'In the early days, I was his personal assistant,' she said, as a wistful expression crossed her face. 'It was all typing and phone calls and arranging meetings. There weren't even computers! And the day didn't finish at five o'clock. No, sometimes we were there till almost midnight.'

I wondered if there could have been some kind of romance between Lydia and Alex.

It was possible. Relationships happened between people in close quarters. Kim was obviously wondering the same thing. 'There was Mrs Carlyle,' she said.

'Yes?' Lydia said icily.

Kim continued. 'It's hard to believe Alex had the time for

family.'

Lydia nodded slowly. 'It was hard for him,' she said. 'Mister Carlyle needed a good woman at his side, and she was it. Loyal. Supportive. A wonderful mother to the children.'

I spoke up. 'Yesterday, we discussed how she'd died in a home invasion. A botched robbery. Was that here?'

'In the old house.'

'How did it happen?'

'I don't know the details. You'd have to ask the police.'

She was holding back. Was there more to Lucy Carlyle's death than she was letting on?

'Last night,' I started, 'I heard you and Allen speaking.'

'When?'

'Around two o'clock.'

'Why were you nosing about?'

I forced a smile. 'You remember I needed a glass of water?' I said. 'I heard your voices in the kitchen. Then Simon came crashing down the stairs.'

'We were talking about a medical issue.'

'Concerning Alex?' Kim asked.

'No.'

'So it was about...'

The woman's eyes flashed with fury. 'Health!' she snapped. 'My health, if you must know. I have cancer!'

My mind went back to the conversation:

'...haven't got long anyway. Surely there's another way?'

'It's necessary.'

'But the end is coming soon.'

Lydia's diagnosis must have been serious. It could even be terminal. We mumbled our apologies. 'I'm so sorry to hear that,' I said. 'Doctor Shipley seems like a good doctor.'

'He's excellent. If you don't have any more questions—'

'Just one or two.' I pushed on. 'The man who killed Alex left the building via the rear servant's stairs. He jumped from a window?'

'Those stairs haven't been used in years. They've always been locked, as far as I know. The door at the bottom is locked, as is the one leading into Mister Carlyle's room.'

'Where does it lead?'

'The garage.'

That was where I'd heard Jasmine talking.

'How do you think the killer gained access to the house?'

'I have no idea.'

'Really?' Kim spoke up. 'That front door is pretty solid. How would he get in?'

Lydia gave a tiny shrug. 'We've had dozens of tradespeople over the years,' she said. 'Keys have gone missing. Anyone could have stolen them.' She glanced at her watch. 'Now, I need to get back to work. People still need feeding. The house still needs to be run. Mister Carlyle would have wanted that.

Now, was there anything else?'

Yes, a million things, although I needed time to process what Lydia had said. We thanked her and went upstairs. The police were still filing in and out of Alex's section of the house. Kim examined the wall of photos facing the stairs. 'That's a rather odd collection of pictures,' she murmured.

'Alex was known for his rather nasty sense of humour,' I said as we returned to my room. After closing the door behind me, I settled onto the bed with Trixie as Kim sat opposite. 'He was a real practical joker.'

'I wonder how he liked having them played on him.'

'He may not have liked being on the receiving end.'

'Well, if this is a practical joke, it's the best I've ever seen.'

I rubbed my chin. 'I'm wondering what we should do next.'

Kim gasped. 'Rosie,' she said. 'You know who the killer must be?'

'Who?'

'The butler!'

I groaned. 'Kim,' I said. 'Don't be silly. You haven't even met the guy!'

'But the butler's always the killer! And you can see why. They know all the ins and outs of a house and probably harbour long-term resentment about how they've been treated. All that *yes, sir* and *no, sir*.'

'If the guy didn't want to be a butler, then all he had to do was change jobs.'

Kim didn't have a response to this kind of logic, so we went in search of Elliot.

14

The man was leaving the study.

'Elliot!' I said. 'Just in time. Can we have a word?'

'What about, miss?' he asked, his brow creasing.

I told him Alex Carlyle had believed his life was in danger.

'I know all about the snake,' Elliot said. 'I was here the day the parcel arrived. In fact, I took it up to Mister Carlyle's room and handed it to him myself.'

'You didn't notice anything odd?' Kim asked.

Elliot frowned. 'Frankly,' he said, 'I did. The package had an odd weight to it. Something was shifting about in it. At the time, I thought it was a few loose books.'

'And Alex Carlyle still took possession of it?'

'He was always buying books.'

'Then what happened?'

'I left Mister Carlyle and went back downstairs to answer the door. Doctor Shipley had arrived to give Mister Carlyle his daily examination. We were halfway up the stairs when

Mister Carlyle started yelling. We raced into the room.' Elliot shuddered. 'That's when we saw the snake. It was huddled up in a corner. Fortunately, Mister Carlyle had the good sense to throw the box away when he saw what it contained. Doctor Shipley killed the snake with a fire poker.'

I was suspicious. 'Allen Shipley just happened to be here when the snake turned up,' I said.

'The doctor comes here every day.'

Kim spoke up. 'You worked for Alex Carlyle for a long time?' she said.

'Thirty-four years,' he said.

Goodness, I thought. *Alex must have inspired some kind of incredible loyalty.*

'As a butler?' I said.

'As a driver, initially.' Elliot looked embarrassed saying it. 'For about half that time, just a driver.'

'And you became a butler...'

'Mister Carlyle needed someone to assist him more and more as the years passed. Over the last seventeen years or so, I also took on the role of butler. There's a training college in London that Mister Carlyle sent me to. Paid for my education. I returned as a butler and have worked in the role ever since.'

'And you still drove as well?' I asked, thinking back to the incident I'd had with Alex over the parking spot.

'Mister Carlyle could drive. He enjoyed it, actually. Having a driver allowed him to work when we went places.' He paused. 'Incidentally, Mister Carlyle could still walk, although only short distances.'

I didn't know that.

'And you liked being a butler?' Kim asked.

For one brief instant, a flicker of something passed in Elliot's eyes. He must have realised we'd noticed because he gave the tiniest of shrugs. 'It's a job,' he said. 'And I was paid well.'

'Alex Carlyle was a difficult man,' I said.

'He didn't suffer fools gladly. If someone was competent, he appreciated and retained them. Others, he got rid of.'

'And his children?'

Elliot frowned. 'I don't know what you mean?'

'You must have known Mister Carlyle's children for a long time. Their entire lives, I suppose.'

'I had little to do with them when they were growing up. They went to boarding school, and I exclusively drove Mister Carlyle. Later, when I transitioned into the position of butler, I rarely saw them.'

'They didn't like visiting?' Kim asked.

'Appointments were made with Lydia. She would know more about that than me.'

Goodness, I thought. *So they had to make appointments with their own father.*

'What will you do now?' I asked.

For the first time, Elliot looked lost. 'I'm not sure, madam,' he said. 'I know Mister Carlyle has left a small sum in his will for me. I can buy a house, I suppose. Other than that, travel, possibly. It's hard to say. This is all quite unexpected.'

We thanked Elliot for speaking to us. What I wanted to do now was begin interviewing Alex's children. However, Todd and Constable Turner were still dealing with them. We found Doctor Shipley leaving for his car.

'So Alex told you about the snake,' Allen said, nodding. 'I thought he might. He knew someone wanted to kill him.'

'We understand you were here when the parcel arrived,' I said.

'I killed it,' he said, shuddering. 'Horrible thing. I've never liked snakes.'

'How did you become Alex's doctor?' Kim asked.

Allen laughed. 'That was another close call for Alex,' he said. 'Someone sideswiped him as he was crossing the road. Missed him by inches. Left him shaken. I happened to pass by a few moments later and gave him something to calm his nerves. He offered me a job on the spot.'

'How long ago was that?' I asked.

'Three years.' Allen Shipley thought, frowning. 'I've never really thought too seriously about it, but now I wonder about that accident—if it were an accident.'

'You think it could have been another murder attempt?'

'Possibly.'

'Did anyone get a look at the driver?' Kim asked.

'Unfortunately not.'

I nodded. 'You saw the man that Jasmine spotted from the window?' I asked.

'Just for a second,' Allen said. 'I saw him again, though, when we all went on that mad dash through the woods.'

'What did he look like?'

'Glasses. Thin build. Losing his hair. I only glimpsed him for a moment, though. The police asked me for a description, and I couldn't help much.'

'I didn't see anyone,' I said, thinking. 'Allen, I do want to ask you about Lydia. She told us about her illness and that you were helping her.'

Allen hesitated. 'I can't share details about a patient's health,' he said. 'It's a breach of patient confidentiality.'

'But she has cancer?'

'I'm sorry, Rosie. I really can't say.'

'It seems strange that Lydia wanted to see you at that hour.'

'I've known Lydia for a few years,' he said. 'It was her choice to meet at that time. Again, it was a matter of confidentiality, and I really can't say anything more than that.'

It was an odd time for a doctor's appointment. Of course, Lydia was a strange woman. Maybe she wanted to keep her illness quiet. If Doctor Shipley was visiting the house all the time, it was likely he would become her physician.

But a doctor's appointment in the middle of the night...

Allan said he had to leave, and we thanked him for his time. He drove off, and we returned inside. 'Maybe we can finally chat with one of Alex's children,' I said.

It turned out that speaking to the three siblings was out of the question as Todd was still interviewing them. However, he'd finished with Jasmine, and we hurried after her. I introduced Kim.

'This has been such an awful day,' Jasmine said.

'I suppose you've known Alex for a long time,' I said.

'Ten years. Ever since I've known Simon.'

'It must be a terrible shock, although Alex wasn't an easy person.'

Jasmine gave a bitter laugh. 'There's no need to beat about the bush,' she said. 'Everyone felt the same way about him: he was universally hated.' She shook her head. 'And then he had that twisted sense of humour.'

I remembered the photos on the first-floor landing wall. 'He seemed to like having fun at other people's expense,' I said.

'And sometimes his little jokes went horribly wrong.' She pointed to her scar. 'You see this? Happened as a result of one of Alex's practical jokes.'

15

'What?' I said.

She nodded. 'Alex gave a wrapped present to Simon,' she explained. 'It was a few years back, just before Christmas. Said he'd given Simon something special. Well, it was special, all right. Simon slid back the lid, and a knife catapulted out.'

'That's terrible!' Kim said.

'It was purposely made to miss him. Alex hadn't intentionally wanted to harm Simon.' She grimaced. 'It was supposed to be like one of those knives in the old movies. Narrowly misses the victim. The problem is that the knife catapulted out at the wrong angle and hit me in the face.'

'Jasmine,' Kim said. 'It's barely noticeable, although I am wondering…'

'Why didn't I have plastic surgery to repair the skin? I've kept it as a reminder. My own little jab back at Alex so that whenever he laid eyes on me, he'd think back to his stupid joke.'

'You spied the killer from the window,' I said. 'Can you describe him?'

Jasmine thought. 'I've already been through this with the police,' she said. 'And I don't think I can be of much help. I only saw him at a distance and then just for a moment. He was tall with thick glasses. Maybe with thinning hair and slim build.' She frowned. 'Although, frankly, he did look vaguely familiar.'

'A business associate of Alex Carlyle's?' Kim suggested.

'I don't know. As I say, I only saw him for a second, and then he was gone.'

I thought back to the dinner. 'Alex mentioned the properties you and Simon own,' I said. 'In Briarbrook.'

'Oh yes,' Jasmine said bitterly. 'The units. How I wish we'd never bought those places. Alex told us not to, although they seemed a good investment at the time. The problem is that we put most of our money into them.'

'You made money on them for a while?'

'We did. At first, they chugged on, producing rental income, and all was fine. Then a tenant started complaining about rising damp and mould. It turned out to be in most of the units. Getting the brickwork replaced would cost a fortune, and the insurance company wouldn't cover it. At the same time, we had a problem with plumbing in the other building. The pipes were bad. We knew that when we bought the place.

We just didn't realise how bad. There was a huge leak that flooded most of the building. Again, insurance wouldn't cover it.' She shook her head in dismay. 'Everything went wrong.'

I felt for her. Sometimes life didn't go according to plan. My thoughts returned to the conversation at the dinner table.

'Alex mentioned a social media platform,' I said. 'You put some money into.'

'Surfacery,' she said. 'Sorry, it's still painful to talk about.'

'Business is hard,' Kim sympathised. 'I have a cousin who created a diet scheme where you ate only brussels sprouts. Turns out people don't like brussels sprouts.'

'Wow,' I said. 'Who knew?'

Jasmine continued. 'It was my brother's company,' she said. 'Surfacery used deep fake technology to make you look like anyone. Then you could use the platform to communicate with others. Although Alex said we didn't have a lawyer to advise us, we did. We were given bad advice.'

'Now that Alex is dead,' I said, 'Who inherits?'

'I don't know. Until recently, Simon was the main beneficiary, but you saw how Alex behaved. He was constantly changing his will. Playing the siblings against each other. For all I know, the money's going to a cat's home.'

We need to find out, I thought, *who inherits?*

'I want to ask you about last night,' I said. 'I heard you in the garage. You were speaking to someone.'

Jasmine frowned. 'It wasn't me,' she said. 'I was sound asleep.'

'But I definitely heard you.'

The woman hesitated. 'Oh,' she said, reddening. 'It could have been me. When I can't sleep, I habitually get up at night and talk to myself. It helps me collect my thoughts.'

That's the weakest excuse I've ever heard.

'Jasmine—' I began.

'Now I really need to lie down,' Jasmine cut in. 'It's been a terrible day and I have to rest.'

Thanking her, Kim and I went back downstairs. Kim We exchanged glances.

'Jasmine talks to herself in the middle of the night?' Kim said.

'Ridiculous,' I said. 'I wonder who she was really talking to. It wasn't her husband. She would have admitted it.'

'Then who could it be?'

At that moment, Rani emerged from the east wing, looking shell-shocked.

'Rani?' I said.

The woman opened her mouth to speak but then burst into tears. I gave her a big hug before pulling back and introducing Kim.

'I'm sorry,' Rani sniffed. 'I don't normally do that in front of people I don't know.'

'Can we talk?' I asked. 'I know it's been an upsetting day...'

'Outside?' she suggested. 'I need to get out of here.'

We left the castle, crossed the bridge, and were soon out in the field. It seemed like days had passed since I'd joined the others on that mad scramble through the forest. By now, the sun was high in the sky, and my stomach was starting to grumble.

'I know this has been a terrible day,' I began. 'You've just lost your father.'

Rani gave a bitter laugh. 'The worst part is I don't know whether to grieve or to celebrate. You probably noticed my father wasn't the easiest person to know.'

'He was difficult.'

'I know I'll miss him. That's the most awful part. It's like missing an abuser because that's all he was to us. He would grudgingly help and, at the same time, crush us every chance he got.'

'He was critical of your business as an influencer,' I said.

'Which was typical of him. He didn't understand how that kind of business works.'

Kim spoke up. 'Can you explain it to me?' she asked. 'I don't quite understand it either.'

Rani sighed. 'There's a lot of ways that influencers gain a social media following,' she said. 'One is simply by getting famous in some quirky manner. Maybe they've appeared on a lifestyle program or been accidentally caught up in a big news story. Another is by instructing or educating people in something. My speciality is makeup.' She hesitated. 'But it takes time to build a following. That's what Daddy...' Tears filled her eyes. 'That's what he couldn't understand.'

I spoke gently. 'Your father said something about buying followers in Nigeria?' I said.

'That's common,' Rani said, waving away the issue. 'I now have ten thousand legitimate followers, with more joining every day. A video where I lip-synced to a Gosi Romero song while applying Chanel blush went viral and got over a hundred thousand views.'

She seemed to be recovering quite quickly from the tragedy of her father's death. In fact, talking about her business was rapidly banishing the tears from her eyes. I asked her about seeing the killer in the forest.

'I only caught a glimpse of him,' she said.

'Can you describe him?' Kim asked.

The woman shook her head. 'Not well.' She hesitated. 'Tallish, I suppose. Glasses. Losing his hair. Skinny.'

'Rani,' I began. 'When I got up during the night, I heard you talking to someone in the library.'

Rani stopped walking. 'Really?' she said. 'Me?'

'Yes. It was you. Who were you talking to?'

'No one,' she said defensively. 'I mean...I sometimes talk to myself to get my ideas straight.'

Good grief! I thought. *What is it with these people?*

'Really?' I continued. 'Because you mentioned something about being *only a matter of time* and *caring about someone.* What was all that about?'

'Oh.' Rani shrugged. 'Nothing. Just practicing for one of my videos. I do that all the time.'

There wasn't much I could do to break down her story. I'd tell Todd, and maybe he could get the truth from her. By now, we'd rounded the entire castle and had arrived back at the front entrance. Rani glanced at her watch and told us she had to leave. Without giving us a chance to reply, she arrowed for her car and was soon driving away from the castle. She disappeared into the surrounding forest.

'Wow,' Kim said. 'That's the fastest escape I've ever seen.'

'You notice it happened right after I asked about her talking to someone last night?'

'You're not wrong there. Talk about *liar, liar, pants on fire!* What is it with these people?'

'They're the worst liars I've ever met.' Trixie whined, and I gave her a pat. 'Even Trixie knew she was lying.'

'I wonder who she was talking to,' Kim said.

'I don't know, but something is up with these people.'

'Let's find out what.'

16

We spotted Lachlan as soon as we re-entered the castle. He looked tired and still in shock, but he was prepared to speak with us. After I introduced Kim, we headed up to his room where we took seats while he sat on his bed.

'It's been a long day,' he said, rubbing his unshaven face. 'I hope you'll excuse me if I'm a bit vague. My brain is running on overdrive.'

'That's understandable,' I said. 'How did it go with Todd Parker?'

'The policeman? As well as can be expected. He asked us what we saw.'

'And you saw the killer?' Kim said. 'What did he look like?'

Lachlan rubbed his chin. 'I only saw him momentarily,' he said. 'Just a flash of him in the trees as he ran. He could really move, by the way. Must be a runner judging by his pace.'

'Can you give us any kind of description?' I asked.

'He was older, I guess. Glasses. Skinny. Losing his hair.'

'Tall?'

'I suppose so. Yes. Tall.'

'I know today has been terrible,' I said. 'But last night was difficult too. The dinner...'

The man gave a bitter laugh. 'Another fun night at Carlyle Castle,' he said. 'I'm sorry you were privy to that. My father never minded washing our dirty laundry out in public.'

'He was a difficult man.'

'You should have been a diplomat rather than a reporter. I think it's safe to say that our father hated everyone. That included us, although he couldn't come out and say it. I think it was his childhood that made him so disagreeable. Craig Carlyle was a terrible man and made his son just as bad.'

I nodded. It was an old story. Sometimes it wasn't easy for children to outgrow their parent's legacy.

'Your father commented on your business,' I said. 'You're a carpenter?'

'Yes.' Lachlan smirked. 'The great Alex Carlyle saw that as being beneath me. Beneath the Carlyle name. Or maybe it was because I enjoyed it, and that's what he really hated. I was satisfied. Finally satisfied.'

Kim spoke up. 'Have you had other businesses?' she asked.

'More than a few,' Lachlan admitted. 'And it was always with my father's encouragement. He bankrolled all of them. Looking back now, I wish he hadn't. Every time I used his money to try to start a business, the thing went sour. I tried opening a café. That went belly-up. Then I went into real estate, got my license, and found I couldn't sell houses if my life depended on it.' He let out a long breath. 'It was one disaster after another. Every time I failed, my father berated me and made me feel less. Finally, I remembered what I loved doing in high school: carpentry. I helped out on a building site and—despite being older—got offered an apprenticeship.

'I think it irked my father that I was happy. I wasn't trying to follow in his footsteps. I'd rejected his dream for my own dream. And you know what?' Lachlan peered at us. 'I was happy. For the first time in years, I was happy.'

I fixed my gaze on Lachlan. 'You did mention your father's money last night,' I reminded him. 'You said it was so much money that you could have anything you wanted.'

'And I meant it. I still do.' He frowned. 'I don't know who's getting the money. Simon, I suppose, unless Dad had already changed his will.'

'Will Simon share the inheritance?'

'I doubt it. Money's like that. Oh, I'm sure he'll give us a few crumbs, but mostly he'll forget that we even exist.' Lachlan shook his head. 'It's strange, you know, now that the old man's gone, I'll miss him. Maybe that's how it is with abusers. You love and hate them all at once.'

'Lachlan,' Kim said. 'Can I ask you again about the man you

all chased through the forest? You've never seen him before?'

'Funny you should say that.' Lachlan frowned in thought. 'I did have a vague idea that I recognised him. No idea where from, though.' He glanced at his watch. 'Look, I'm sorry. I'd better get moving. I had some messages on my phone that I've got to attend to.'

We thanked him for his time. We were about to leave when he hesitated. 'Actually, Rosie,' he continued. 'Can I get your contact details? In case we need to chat further?'

I handed Lachlan my card. Wishing us a good day, he grabbed his bag, and we walked out with him to the courtyard, where he drove off and disappeared into the woods. I turned to Kim who was grinning.

Huh?

'I've obviously missed something,' I said.

'You didn't notice the way he was staring at you?'

'No. I think he was just...looking. You know how people open their eyes and look at things?'

She punched my arm. 'You idiot!' she said. 'He was giving you the eye! And look at him! He's a hot guy!'

I was about to tell Kim that she was imagining things when I thought back to Lachlan's eyes. He *had* been looking at me. Quite fixedly, now that I thought about it. And he'd just asked for my contact details. I could have slapped myself.

Sometimes, I'm thick!

'Well,' I said, considering. 'He *is* good-looking.'

'And available, by the look of it: no wedding ring.'

Lachlan wasn't married, as far as I knew. Or seeing anyone. But there was an obstacle.

'What about Todd?' I asked.

'What about him?' Kim asked, exasperated. 'Todd's a great guy, but he's had a million opportunities to ask you out on dates. He could have disembarked from the all-stations train to Friendsville and climbed aboard the express service to Rosieland.' She pointed at me. 'And he hasn't. You know that old saying? A bird in the hand…'

I suppose Kim was right. As much as I liked Todd—some might even call it love—he'd never given a serious indication of our friendship being more than that: friendship. We went back inside just as Simon emerged from the library. He arrowed over to us.

'Rosie,' he said. 'We need to talk.'

'Okay.' This was a change. Most people tried to stay away from reporters. I quickly introduced Kim. 'What is it?'

'Can we chat somewhere?'

We went to the billiard room, where Simon slumped into one of the comfortable chairs. The poor man looked like he hadn't slept in weeks. The stench of alcohol came off him in waves. I wondered how he survived.

'It's that police officer,' Simon began. 'He seems determined to pin this thing on me.'

'What do you mean?' I asked.

'It was that comment I made at dinner. I meant nothing by it, but that policeman seems to have taken it to heart.'

I thought back to the dinner. So many tactless things had been said that it was hard to keep track. Then I remembered.

'I hate him,' Simon had seethed. 'I wish he were dead!'

I tactfully shared this with Kim, who nodded sympathetically. 'People say that kind of thing,' she said. 'I've got a cousin who used to say that all the time to her husband. She must have said it a hundred times over the years.' Kim considered. 'Mind you, she ended up running him over with a tractor.'

'Well, I didn't kill my father!' Simon cried, his face a mixture of shock and horror. 'I loved him! Well, as much as anyone could love him. He was a...complicated man.'

To my mind, the word *complicated* was often a euphemism for *awful*. 'Simon,' I said. 'I was at the dinner with you and the others.' I hesitated. 'I can't imagine what it was like living with him.'

Simon's face crumpled. 'He was ghastly! Terrible!' Simon looked ready to burst into tears. 'You can't know what it was like growing up in that house. My father was a bully. He would chastise us at every opportunity. The only saving grace was our mother. Without her, I don't know how we would have survived.'

'I remember her painting,' I said. 'She was gorgeous.'

'Our mother was an American actress. Starred in several Broadway shows. I don't know if you remember her.'

'I'm afraid I don't.'

'It was years ago now. Back then, she was on the verge of hitting it big. Really big.' Simon's face darkened. 'That's when she met my father. He was much older, of course. Normally didn't go to the theatre. He didn't like entertainment at all. A waste of time, he thought. But he was in New York on business when a client paid for them to see a show. The man knew Lucy, and they later visited her backstage.' Simon shrugged. 'What can I say? She loved my father. I don't know why. They were married three months after they met.'

'Simon,' Kim said carefully. 'Your father was quite wealthy. Is it possible—'

'—that my mother married him for his money? I wish it were that simple. It wasn't that. For some reason, she loved him, and he loved her. People have told me that he wasn't so difficult after that. For a while. And then when she died, he became harder than ever.'

'It must have been difficult for him,' I said. 'She died in a botched robbery?'

'We were away at a friend's place. Father was on a business trip. It was terrible. There was a call the next morning. Lydia found her body. Jewellery was missing. Our mother had been struck over the head. Died almost instantly.'

'Simon,' Kim began. 'Can you give us a description of the man you saw? The man in the woods?'

He shrugged. 'Thin,' he said, thinking. 'Balding. Black-rimmed glasses. Other than that, I don't know. I only saw him for a moment. He was really moving.'

I wanted to ask more questions, but the door eased open at that moment and Jasmine appeared. 'Simon,' she said. 'You're finished with the police?'

He nodded. 'Statement made,' he said. 'All done.'

'Then we need to go.'

Simon looked like a helpless child as he nodded. 'You're right, darling,' he said. 'Of course, you're right.' He turned to us. 'None of this has gone as anyone planned. I'm sorry, Rosie. You've seen us all at our worst.'

'It's a difficult time,' I said. 'Can we talk to you later if needed?'

'Of course.'

Simon handed us a card, and he and Jasmine left.

'Wow,' Kim said. 'That's everyone interviewed.'

I nodded. 'Now let's see Todd,' I said. 'And find out how the killer stormed a supposedly impregnable castle!'

17

'It's a locked room mystery,' Todd said. 'And I don't like locked room mysteries.'

'Well, I love them,' I said. 'Although, not when they involve someone's death.'

Trixie whined.

'I'm with Trixie,' Kim said. 'Locked room mysteries: good. Murder: bad.'

Kim, Todd, and I were standing in the middle of Alex Carlyle's vast room. His body had been taken away, although his wheelchair remained in the same position. A sad trace of his death was the blanket he'd worn over his knees. I remembered looking at the old man and thinking he hadn't long to live.

Well, I was right about that.

I hadn't taken much notice of this room before, but now I examined it more closely.

It was a single vast chamber, illuminated by six windows set high into the stonework. Tapestries decorated the walls.

Although they appeared to be ancient, I suspected they were for appearances only. A lot of things about this castle were like that.

The walls were stone. The floor was stone too, other than some timber panelling. The massive bed at the far end of the room had caught my attention the first time I'd entered, and it did again now. It was huge. Bigger than king size. I suppose Alex Carlyle spent a lot of time in bed and decided to make himself as comfortable as possible.

I glanced over at the lounge. I'd been sitting on that lounge less than a day before, and Alex had told me someone wanted to kill him. He'd asked me to keep an eye on everyone, and I had. And what had I learned?

So far—nothing.

'Todd,' Kim said. 'I thought the killer escaped via a window down the servants' stairs?'

'That's true. The problem is how he did that.' Todd crossed to the door on the other side of the room. 'This door was locked from the inside with this bolt.' He indicated the latch. 'If that isn't bad enough, there's a second door at the bottom of the stairs. That's locked too.'

I slowly put this together in my head. 'Hang on,' I said. 'The door leading from the common hall landing was locked as well. And yet the killer came through this way and escaped out the window. Which means...' *Oh dear.* 'The only person who could have relocked this door was Alex Carlyle.'

'Which is unlikely,' Todd said. 'Seeing as how the man had a knife in his left eye, his hands were tied behind his back, and he was gagged. The blade impacted his brain, causing almost instantaneous death. It's unlikely that even an able-bodied person would have lived more than a few seconds.'

'And even if they did,' Kim said, 'locking doors is probably not going to be a priority.'

Todd nodded. 'You see my problem.'

I gazed around the room. 'Mind if we take a look?'

'Be my guest.'

Kim and I crossed to the door that we had come through earlier. The lock was an old-fashioned sliding bolt, thick and made of iron. No wonder it had taken so much effort to smash through. The bolt had been placed into a clear evidence bag.

'It was the catch plate that gave way,' Todd explained. 'Tore straight out of the timber.'

'We were lucky to get through as quickly as we did,' I said. 'But how did the killer get in? This would have been locked?'

'According to the butler, Alex Carlyle locked it every night. In fact, the butler even heard him secure it after he left.'

'I suppose someone else could have knocked at the door, and Alex reopened it for them.'

Crossing to the other door, we examined the bolt and found it almost identical to the one on the main door. Unlike that one, however, this was intact. We continued past it and entered a tiny hall about ten feet long. A door led off from one side to a surprisingly modern bathroom. We glanced inside. Light came in through one of the tiniest sash windows I'd ever seen. It barely measured a foot across.

No one came or went through there, I thought.

We continued down the hallway. A window on our right was larger than the one in the bathroom but did not open.

Kim spoke up. 'Can you show us the window the killer jumped from?' she asked.

We went down a narrow flight of stone stairs. Despite being illuminated by old bulbs strung along the ceiling, the stairwell still seemed dark and closed in. We reached the window halfway down the stairs. The sash window was raised, and I saw scuff marks on the sill. The floor under the window was wet from the previous night's storm.

'It looks like he stepped onto the sill,' Todd said, 'to leap into the water.'

Kim and I peered down. It was a drop of about ten feet into deep water. Although the splash would have been loud, it was unlikely anyone would have heard it from inside the building.

'Everyone said the killer wore glasses,' I said. 'They must have been superglued to his head.'

'He may have stuck them in his pocket and put them back on when he ran across the field,' Todd said.

'This water on the floor is confusing, too,' I said. 'Do you know what time it stopped raining during the night?'

'I've already checked the satellite maps. A storm came in from the west after midnight. By three o'clock, the front had moved on, and the rest of the night was dry.'

'Then this window was opened before three.'

'Alex's body was still warm,' Todd confirmed. 'The police examiner can give us a more exact time of death, but it looks like he died not long before you broke in the door.'

'This is odd. The rain on the floor means the killer arrived sometime before three to open this window. He stayed until breakfast when we found Alex's body. What was he doing all that time? Talking to Alex? Trying to get information from him? Why did he wait all that time to kill him?' I peered down the stairs. 'Where do these lead?'

We followed Todd down to a timber door at the far end. Todd showed us the locking mechanism. 'This was locked from this side when we arrived,' Todd said. 'Which just adds to the conundrum. This door was locked, and so was the one leading from the upstairs landing.'

'And Alex Carlyle was largely wheelchair-bound. I assume Elliot told you Alex was capable of some walking?'

'Yes. The doctor confirmed it too. But Alex could only walk about half a dozen paces. Not down a flight of stairs.'

We pushed through into an underground cellar where food

supplies lined timber shelves on both walls and continued to a set of stairs at the end which led up into another room. Climbing the stairs, we emerged into the garage where Alex Carlyle's grey Mercedes was now parked. A forensics officer was fingerprinting the garage's side door.

'I can make a guess at whose fingerprints he might find,' I said. 'Jasmine. Maybe even the mysterious person she was talking to.'

Todd nodded. 'I asked her about coming down here, and she gave me some weak excuse about talking to herself.'

'She told us that too,' I said, shaking my head. 'Pathetic.'

'So what was she doing here?'

'Meeting someone,' Kim said. 'But who?'

'Whoever it was,' I said, 'it doesn't look good. You don't meet someone in a cold, dusty garage at two in the morning to swap recipes.' I thought. 'It could be Simon, although I have no idea why she'd come down here to speak to him. She could do that in her room anytime.'

'Who else is there?' Kim asked. 'Rani?'

'Not Rani,' I said. 'She was in the library also talking to someone.'

'Then Allen or Lydia?' Todd suggested. 'You said they were both in the kitchen.'

'They're both a possibility,' I admitted. 'I was in the billiard room while Rani was speaking to someone. It could have been

Allen and Lydia. After she left, they could have gone to the kitchen, and she went upstairs. Later, I came out of the billiard room and was listening to Allen and Lydia in the kitchen when Simon fell down the stairs.'

'All right,' Kim said thoughtfully. 'There's Lachlan.'

'Hmm,' I nodded. 'Now that puts an interesting perspective on things. Could Lachlan and Jasmine—'

'—be having an affair?' Todd said. 'That would be quite messy, as she's his sister-in-law.'

'Stranger things have happened,' I said.

Kim was smiling strangely. 'But you know who this leaves?'

I groaned. 'Kim, not the butler?'

'Yes!' she said. 'The butler! It's always the butler!'

Even Todd rolled his eyes. 'Kim,' he said. 'I've been a cop for a long time, and I've never arrested a butler for murder yet.'

'Yeah? How many have you met?'

Even Todd was stumped by this. 'Okay,' he said. 'We'll agree that Jasmine could have been conspiring with Elliot for some reason. But there's one final person that Jasmine could have been speaking to, and that's the killer.'

Kim and I nodded. 'Jasmine could be working with the killer,' I agreed. 'She could have even let him into the building.'

'Except,' Kim said, 'anyone could have let him into the building. And it doesn't seem likely the killer came in this way. If he did, he relocked the door after entering.'

Todd led us back into the tunnel and up the servant's stairs. 'So the killer enters via the front door, probably using a key that he's acquired at some time in the past. He goes to Alex's door, and the old man lets him in for some strange reason. Once inside, he binds and gags the old man—'

'—and opens the window on the back stairs,' Kim said. 'Don't forget the rainwater on the floor.'

'True.' We continued into Alex's chamber. 'Once here, he relocks the door and waits several hours before killing him. Then, after the murder, he returns to the back stairs, magically relocking that door behind him.'

'Could someone else have relocked the door?' I asked.

'I asked everyone,' Todd said. 'The answer was a collective no. Besides, everyone went chasing after the killer. They're hardly going to be up here locking doors.'

'So what's the answer?' Kim asked.

The three of us stared at the door in question.

Who relocked the door after the murder?

18

We began by checking the walls around the room. I'd found secret staircases in buildings before, and I was sure that would be the case here. There had to be a second way from this room to the stairwell. After all, people couldn't pass through solid doors.

The panelling on the walls was some kind of faux mahogany. The styling was plain except for the bookcases and the fireplace surrounds which had ornate patterning around them.

We felt along every crevice and crack, searching for the slightest movement, and pressed and pulled on every decorative feature in the stonework.

After an hour of doing this, we turned our attention to the floor. This was made of enormous paving stones, a tan and yellow sandstone which abutted tightly against each other across the length and breadth of the floor.

By now, we were growing grimly desperate. We returned to the bookcases and started removing books, but Todd soon called a halt to this process.

'Ladies,' he said, peering up at the high shelves. 'There's no way the killer could have replaced these books, even if he did escape this way.'

Todd was right. 'Okay,' I said. 'That would seem to leave the ceiling.'

'And the fireplace itself,' Kim pointed out. 'The killer could have climbed up the chimney and onto the roof. He could have jumped from there into the moat.'

'Maybe,' I said. 'But that's quite a jump. And what about the open window on the landing?'

'A red herring?'

It was possible. 'Let's rule out one thing at a time,' I said. 'First, the ceiling. Is there any way someone could reach it to escape via a secret hatch?'

The ceiling was fifteen feet high. A chandelier hung from the middle of the room, with recessed lights added to provide additional lighting. The only way to get to the ceiling was to scale the chandelier.

'Which is basically impossible,' Todd pointed out. 'I doubt the chain holding the chandelier would support a person's weight. Even if it did, where do you go once you get to the top?'

There weren't any apparent joins in the ceiling that could peel back to reveal an exit. And if such an exit existed, how could the killer have gotten to it?

'What's above that ceiling?' I asked.

'The roof,' Todd said, 'which is surprisingly inaccessible. You can only get up there via a trapdoor in the ceiling above the main stairs.'

I sighed. 'Even if there's a hidden panel in that ceiling, a person would have to be an acrobat to reach it,' I mused. 'Or trapeze artist.'

Kim was nodding enthusiastically. 'Elliot was previously a chauffeur,' she said. 'But what did he do before that?'

'Good question,' I said. 'Was he a trapeze artist? Maybe he walked a tightrope in a circus.'

'Do you think?'

'No! You dummy!' I punched her arm. 'The guy probably worked in a shop or filed reports in an office.'

Kim pulled a face. 'We still need to check—and let's not forget the chimney.'

Todd was trying not to smile. 'Okay, Kim,' he said. 'I'll check to see if Elliot ever worked as a trapeze artist. It's a shame I didn't ask him earlier.'

'Now you're giving me a hard time too!'

'Not at all. For the moment, let's rule out the trapeze artist butler theory. That's a good point about the chimney, though.'

We peered into and up the chimney, although this quickly proved to be a waste of time.

'Like most chimneys,' I said, 'it has a smoke shelf and a damper.' I pointed to the brickwork that angled up from the back. 'That encourages the smoke towards the damper and up into the flue. The flue is the vertical column through which the smoke rises. The damper is a metal plate like a window that opens to let the smoke out and air in.' I pointed at the metal barrier. 'It's closed now, and no one could fit up there anyway.'

Kim inhaled. 'There's an odd smell here,' she said.

'I noticed that too,' Todd said. 'I thought it was Rosie.'

I punched his arm.

'Ouch!'

'You deserved it!'

'Look,' Kim said, pointing to a pile of goo among the timber in the firebox.

I jabbed it. 'What is that? It looks like burnt rubber.'

'Smells like it, too,' Todd said.

Todd produced an evidence bag and picked up the molten rubber with a pair of tweezers. The rubber was brown and red with splotches of silver.

'That is weird,' Kim said.

Todd put it into the bag. 'Very strange,' he agreed. 'Well spotted, Kim.'

'Thanks.'

'Yes,' I agreed. 'Well done. I almost forgive you for your suggestion about the acrobatic butler.'

Kim chose to ignore me. 'Let's take another look at those doors.'

Kim and I examined it in silence before she dropped to her knees and felt under the door. 'There's a small gap under here,' she said. 'Maybe half an inch.'

A tiny smile played on Todd's lips. 'So the killer was very short?' he suggested.

'No,' I said. 'But I know what Kim's thinking. There have been locked room mysteries where the killer has attached string to the bolt. The door is then shut, and the string angled across to pull the bolt into place.'

'So how is the string removed?' Todd asked.

'It can be a particular type of knot or maybe even a loop. The string is cut from outside the door, which allows it to be removed.' I paused. 'Alternatively, some pretty complex contraptions have been built that do the same thing.'

'That may work in detective stories,' Todd said, 'but this is real life. That's a pretty complicated way to create a locked-room murder. And why do it anyway?'

'Stranger things have happened.'

'What's the gap like under the other door?' Kim asked.

We returned to it and found it was the same size. Could string have been attached to this bolt? Maybe. Although Todd had already touched on a valid point. 'The real question is: why,' I said as we returned to the middle of the room. 'Why create a locked room murder mystery? It's almost like a bad joke.'

'You did say that Alex Carlyle was a practical joker,' Kim said.

'Having himself murdered as a practical joke seems a little extreme. No, this happened for a reason, although I have no idea what that could be. Alex's body was going to be found. The killer's possible routes of escape were always going to be limited. Once the alarm was raised, he decided that jumping into the moat and escaping across the field was his safest course of action.'

There were numerous questions that needed answering. Why had the window on the back stairs been opened hours before? How did the door get relocked after the killing? Why did the killer choose to murder Alex after the sun had risen? Why not murder him during the night and escape under cover of darkness? And how did he even gain entry to the room? Did Alex know his killer? Or did someone from inside the building encourage Alex to open the door?

My head was beginning to hurt. My phone beeped before I could voice some of these questions. I looked down; I had a message from Harry.

I hear there's some action at the castle. What's happening?

I suppressed a smile. Harry had contacts everywhere. No doubt someone had tipped him off. Excusing myself, I went to the landing where I rang him, giving him the news.

'So Alex Carlyle is dead,' Harry said. 'Any suspects?'

'Everyone and no one. It's safe to say that people either hated Alex or were equally happy if he died. The killer created the perfect locked room mystery, although he was spotted escaping to the road. The police are now trying to track him down.'

'The cops are searching the forest?'

'Yes, although it would probably take a hundred cops a month, and they still wouldn't find anything.' This made me think. 'Maybe Kim and I can take a look. I roughly remember the route I took. Maybe I'll find something.'

I returned to the others and told Todd that Kim and I would look around the forest.

'That's fine,' Todd said. 'Just remember—if you find anything, let me know. This is a police investigation. Not a Rosie Ryan adventure.'

'You're no fun,' I told him.

'I'm a cop. I don't have a sense of humour.'

Kim and I left the castle with Trixie and wandered over to the forest. I needed coffee and food, and probably in that order. At the same time, I was aware that finding a clue leading to the killer took precedence. Time was of the essence. Although I remembered the entry point where I'd raced into the forest, it was harder to remember the path of my strange slapdash run.

We wandered through the maze of trees. 'I think I came this

way,' I said after a few minutes.

'You're not sure?' Kim said.

'Not exactly. It was all too crazy.'

Kim turned to Trixie. 'Hey girl,' she said. 'Can you show us the way Rosie came earlier?'

My magnificent beagle turned her head. 'Come on, girl,' I said. 'You can do it.'

She sniffed the air. With a bit of luck...

Trixie bounded decisively through the trees.

Yes!

We trailed after her for several minutes. A few times, she stopped and sniffed the ground before continuing on. Soon we were back on the road. Trixie had done a fantastic job of getting us here, but I wasn't sure we'd learned anything new. Then she trotted further down the road, stopping at a shallow ditch off the road.

'Look,' Kim said. 'She's found something.'

A white plastic card lay in a ditch.

'*Kilkenny Arms*,' I said. 'It's a key card for a hotel room!'

'Could the killer have dropped it?'

'Maybe.' I rubbed Trixie's neck. 'You are such a clever dog. Next thing, I'll train you to get me coffee in the morning.'

Trixie yowled.

'Okay,' I relented. 'Maybe not.'

'Should we tell Todd about this?' Kim asked.

'Not yet. Let's go into town and see what we can discover first.' I paused. 'Except we must drink coffee and eat food first. Otherwise, I won't make it through the day.'

'I'm surprised you've lasted this long.'

'Me too.'

Half an hour later, we staggered in through the front door of the diner, where Sandy took one look at me.

'Let me guess?' Sandy said. 'Coffee?'

'And food. Make it a burger with the lot. Chips. And my usual jumbo-sized caramel latte.'

Kim also ordered food, and we were soon seated with coffee and meals. I took a long sip of my coffee. It was delicious, and my brain immediately came to life.

'I feel guilty,' I told Kim. 'Alex Carlyle told me he feared for his life—and now he's dead.'

Kim sat down her burger. 'He didn't ask you to be his bodyguard.'

'True, but he did ask me to keep an eye on everyone. He was convinced that one of his children wanted to kill him.'

'But the killer appears to be someone outside the family.'

'So it seems.' Taking the hotel key card from my pocket, I peered at it thoughtfully. 'Maybe this will tell us more.'

19

After eating and drinking, I felt a million times better, and we were soon walking through the front entrance of the Kilkenny Arms. Natalie Cook, the blonde-haired manager, was at the counter. She peered down at the key card.

'That's definitely one of ours,' she said.

'Can you tell us who it belongs to?' I asked.

'Has this got to do with Alex Carlyle's murder?' she asked. 'Everyone in town's talking about it.'

'Maybe,' I said carefully. 'Mum's the word for now.'

Nodding, Natalie examined her hotel register. 'Okay,' she said. 'I remember this booking because it was unusual. Henry Sterning is the room hirer, and he's in room four-oh-seven. Supposedly.'

'What do you mean?'

Natalie sighed. 'We received an envelope with a chunk of money in it,' she explained. 'Enough to hire the room for a month. In return, we were asked to send the key card to a postal box.'

'That sound unusual,' Kim said.

'It is.'

'So you don't have any banking details?' I said.

'No,' she said, shaking her head. 'And virtually everything we do these days is via bank transfer.'

'But someone must have seen him while he was here.'

'I know I didn't,' Natalie said, examining her screen. 'Henry Sterning's booking started last Monday. William was working then. You can ask him, if you like.'

A few minutes later, we were talking to William in the bar. He was a pleasant young man, extremely tall with rather big ears. 'Henry Sterning?' he mused. 'Yes, I recall the booking.'

'Can you describe him?'

'I didn't actually see him.'

'Really?' I said, exchanging glances with Kim. 'Not at all?'

'No. Because he never came to the desk.'

Kim spoke up. 'What about the chambermaids?'

It was a good question and one we had an answer to within minutes. None of the chambermaids working that week had spotted the mysterious Henry Sterning. Kim and I returned to Natalie. I explained to her that I'd like to search the room.

She was reluctant. 'Rosie,' she said. 'It's not as if you're officially affiliated with the police. This is a person's private booking we're talking about.'

'Something may have happened to him,' I said. 'A medical episode. He could be unconscious. Or dying.'

I glanced at Kim, who did a barely suppressed eye roll. She'd heard me use the *medical episode* excuse so many times that it was almost a running joke. One day, when I'd been late meeting her for coffee, she'd asked me if it was because I'd suffered a medical episode on the way.

'We can go up there,' Natalie said. 'But please don't touch anything. As I say, the man has rented the room and is entitled to his privacy.'

'Understood,' I promised.

Minutes later, we were inside four-oh-seven. There wasn't much to see. It was neat, with a single bag sitting on the bedside table. The bed was mussed up as if someone had been sleeping in it. A book entitled *Principles of Mathematical Analysis* sat on the bed.

'Well,' Natalie said, clearly uncomfortable. 'It's obvious the man hasn't collapsed. Now that's established, I think we'd best leave.'

My eyes focused on a brochure sitting on the bedside table. *Currumbin Lodge.* It showed a picture of guest cabins in a tiny town five kilometres from the coast.

Is Henry Sterning thinking of leaving?

Thanking her, Kim and I made our way to the footpath outside. A warm breeze swept in from the ocean as we headed to my car.

'So he had the key card sent to a postal box,' Kim said.

'Obviously, to hide his identity. Did you notice that brochure?'

'Currumbin Lodge?'

'Maybe he's also stayed there.'

'Or going to. I think it's worth visiting.'

We were soon on the road to Currumbin. Like so many other Australian towns, it was little more than a dot on a map, albeit a very pretty dot. Nestled within thick bushland, a river bordered the road and the half dozen buildings that comprised the town. We were soon inside the reception area of Currumbin Lodge, where the grey-haired owner behind the counter was listening intently to us.

'Henry Burning?' he muttered. 'Don't know any Henry Burning!'

He was obviously hard of hearing. 'Henry Sterning?' I said loudly. 'He may have stayed here.'

'Oh, yes. He's here.'

Kim and I exchanged glances. 'He's here right now?' Kim said.

'Cabin five.'

'And you've seen him?' I asked.

'Hmm. No. Paid three weeks in advance with cash via the post. You friends of his?'

'Yes, I'm his…sister. He suffers from a medical condition.' I ignored Kim's reaction. 'We need to check on him.'

'Medical condition?' the old man stammered. 'We had a fella die of heart failure in cabin two last year. Stunk up the place terribly. I couldn't rent it for a week after that. Had to use three pine-scented Aroma Domes to put it right.'

'Well,' I said. 'You wouldn't want that.'

The owner led us down a long path through the woods and past a row of tiny timber huts to a solitary building nestled under gum trees. The lake was barely visible through breaks in the trees. I turned to the old man while we were still several feet away.

'I'll do this,' I said. 'Just in case.'

'I'll leave you ladies to it. Let me know if you need anything.'

Kim and I watched the old man toddle back off to his office. 'I'll bet he's checking on his Aroma Domes,' Kim said.

'That's a bet I'd lose,' I replied.

Feeling more than a slight sense of trepidation, I began by knocking on the cabin door. I wasn't sure if I wanted Henry Sterning to be home or not. Kim was obviously feeling the same as she gripped my arm.

'Rosie,' she whispered. 'You know this man is possibly a killer?'

'I know.'

'What do we do if he answers?' She paused. 'Tackle him?

The two of us should be able to take him.'

'*Do not tackle anyone.*' I gave her my fiercest look. 'The man may be completely innocent. I'll explain that we're following up on the death of Alex Carlyle for the Gazette.'

'What if he attacks us?'

'Then we'll tackle him. You go low. I'll go high.'

As it turned out, tackling wasn't required as there was no movement or sound from within the cabin. I peered through the window and saw an empty room with a suitcase on a side table. Carefully unlocking the door, I let us in, and we entered.

'Hello?' I called.

The bathroom door was open. Good. At least a semi-naked man wasn't about to come racing out in surprise.

We conducted a search of the room. Back at the Kilkenny Arms, we'd been unable to conduct a search. Now we could take our time. I checked the contents of the man's suitcase while Kim examined the rest of the room.

It was neatly packed, and the clothing was almost new. There were enough shirts, pants, and underwear for about three days. He'd packed a copy of *Programming in C* by someone named Branford. There were also a few packets of mints and a pair of glasses, and cleaning cloths for the lenses.

The glasses were for someone nearsighted.

Kim emerged from the bathroom. 'Anything?' she asked, and I told her what I'd found. 'There's not much in the bathroom either. Just a hairbrush with some grey hairs.'

'So it looks like Henry is possibly an older man who has an interest in programming. The man wears glasses because he's nearsighted and is planning to stay here for a few days.'

'Except his booking is for three weeks.'

'Yes, that's odd.'

Kim pulled open the drawer of the bedroom table. 'Here's something,' she said. '*Cadda Caravans.*'

'That's not far from here.' I stared at the leaflet. 'Maybe Henry's moved on, and he's at the caravan park.'

'Or maybe he hasn't moved on from any of these places. He might be spreading his time between all three locations to stay on the move.'

It was a good possibility. 'We need to check the caravan park.'

Within minutes, we'd returned the key to the Currumbin Lodge manager and were driving to Cadda. The town was located on a river another fifteen kilometres inland. By now, it was late in the day, with the sun low in the sky, and the day had grown hot. We pulled into the caravan park and made our way to the office. A young girl was behind the counter. She couldn't be any older than fourteen.

'I don't know,' she said when I asked for information about Henry Sterning. 'My dad's out, and I'm not sure we're allowed to give out that kind of information.'

'I'm Henry's sister,' I said.

'Me too,' Kim added.

The girl's eyes zigzagged between the two of us.

'Half-sisters,' I explained. 'Different mothers.'

'Oh.' At that moment, Trixie decided to go to the girl and rub her snout against her knee. 'What a beautiful dog. What kind is she?'

'A beagle.' I continued, delivering my story about my beloved brother having a medical condition and being worried about his health. The girl reluctantly gave me a key to his caravan.

'Try not to be too long,' the girl said, obviously not wanting to get into trouble with her father.

After promising that we'd return as soon as possible, we left the office and weaved through the caravan park to Henry Sterning's caravan. The caravan park was busy with parents and kids everywhere. A stream ran alongside the park with river red gums overhanging the water.

The site number was painted on the road outside each van. A trickle of sweat ran down my back as we reached the van. If Henry Sterning wasn't at either of his other hidey-holes, he may very well be here.

Curtains covered the windows.

'If he answers—' Kim started.

'No tackling,' I said, 'unless I give the word.'

Kim nodded grimly.

I thudded loudly on the door and waited. A group of children raced past us and down to the river with their parents trailing behind. Much to my relief, there was no answer at the door. I shielded my eyes as I peered into a tiny side window.

'No movement,' I reported.

Seconds later, we were inside and searching the caravan. By this stage, I wasn't much surprised to find a similar setup to the other places where Henry was staying. There was another bag, a mix of clothing, and a book. This was a nonfiction volume about castles.

'Good grief,' Kim said, picking up the book. 'This is all rather damning. Not everyone reads books about the history of castles.'

'It doesn't look good,' I agreed, sighing. 'You know what time it is?'

'Time for more food?'

'I was going to suggest speaking to Todd.' I stared at her. 'How do you stay so skinny?'

'Could it be all my running?'

'Either that or a pact with the Devil. No. One thing's pretty clear; Henry Sterning was likely the killer of Alex Carlyle. It's time Todd took over this investigation.'

20

I woke the next morning feeling more than a little deflated. Mysteries usually took several days or weeks to solve. It wasn't often that Kim and I were able to solve them in a day.

I stumbled to the living room where I found Nan doing morning yoga. 'You get any sleep last night?' she asked, peering at me upside-down through her legs.

'Not a lot,' I admitted.

'I could tell. It sounded like you were tossing and turning all night in there.' She winked. 'Dave stayed over last night. We were tossing all night too.'

I groaned. 'Too much information.'

Checking my phone, I saw that Todd had sent me an update.

'Looks like Henry Sterning's been identified as a 'person of interest' in the death of Alex Carlyle,' I told her.

'That's police lingo for *he's guilty though we haven't caught him yet.*'

'Pretty much.'

I got ready, ate some breakfast, and an hour later was arriving at the office. Harry looked up from his desk.

'Good grief,' he said. 'You're here early. Do you never sleep?'

'Not if I can help it. I'm going out for coffee soon, though. Don't expect me to make any sense until I've had my first jumbo double-shot caramel latte for the day.'

'You don't make much sense even after you've had it.'

'Ha-ha. You're a funny guy.'

After checking my emails, I wandered up the road to the diner where Sandy was taking plates of bacon and eggs out to a table of tourists. I followed her inside.

'I heard someone murdered Alex Carlyle,' Sandy said as she frothed the milk for my coffee. 'Must have been hard to work out who. Alex was the most disliked man for hundreds of miles around.'

I nodded. 'Yes,' I said, thinking. 'Still, I got to know him a little when I stayed the other night.'

'And?'

'He was a hard man, though sometimes a hard life does that to a person. Maybe if his life had been easier, he would have been kinder.' Sandy handed me my coffee, and I took a long sip. 'I'm just glad we were able to identify the killer.'

'You should probably open a detective agency,' Sandy said. 'Rosie Ryan: Private Detective.'

'It does have a ring to it,' I agreed. 'But I like writing too much.'

'You started on that book yet?'

I laughed. It was an ongoing conversation that I'd been having with people for years: writing a book. So far, I'd started and stopped half a dozen projects, but nothing ever progressed beyond the third chapter.

'Funny you should ask,' I said. 'I *have* been thinking about a book. A mystery novel.'

Now it was Sandy's turn to laugh. 'Well,' she said. 'You'd be an expert on that.'

I thought about what Sandy said as I returned to the office. I had investigated a bunch of mysteries as part of my job. And an idea for a mystery novel had been brewing in the back of my mind. Maybe it was time to finally write that book...

Back at my desk, I made notes relating to the death of Alex Carlyle. It was only a matter of time before the police tracked down Henry Sterning. He might even be caught by the time the Gazette came out on Friday. I wrote most of the backstory leading up to Alex's death, leaving out the information that Alex had asked me to keep an eye on his children. As far as the end of the story went, I'd leave for Thursday afternoon.

As I was finishing, Harry called out from his office. 'Rosie!' he yelled. 'Are you busy?'

'I'm always busy.'

'Good. If you want anything done, always ask a busy person. Can you head down to the film set? Protesters are down there causing a ruckus.'

'Protesting?' I called back. 'Over the movie?'

'Find out what it's all about. Might be interesting.'

Minutes later, I was driving across town with Trixie. She stuck her head out the window and warm morning air pushed back her ears. Trixie gave a happy bark.

'I know how you feel,' I told her. 'Summer's here, and it'll get a lot warmer before it gets colder.'

We reached the old sports centre and got out. Harry was right. People were marching up and down the footpath outside the main gates. The cops had arrived, although the protestors seemed peaceful. People were holding up hand-written signs adorned with pictures of cats. *Save Our Cats* and *Felines Have Rights Too!* were just a few. Pulling over, I immediately spotted a familiar face.

'Wanda?' I said, hurrying over to her. 'What's happening?'

Wanda Gibson was a member of the Cape Carson Mystery Book Club. She was also a keen lover of cats and owned a walnut-coloured Abyssinian named Bastet. The woman was now holding a sign aloft with a picture of a cat dressed in a party hat.

'Rosie!' she boomed. 'Thank goodness you're here! We need media attention on this.'

'Uh...on what?'

'The abuse of these poor cats, of course.' Wanda lowered her sign. 'Have you heard what they're doing? Dressing up cats like runway models and forcing them to prance and dance around for people's amusement. It's obscene!'

I hadn't quite thought about it that way. Taking out my notepad, I turned to a new page. 'So you believe it's abusive to cats?' I said.

'Cats are living creatures,' Wanda said. 'They have the right to not be made to look foolish.'

'And that's what the movie is doing?'

'Did they ask the cats if they wanted to be dressed up? No. Instead, their owners have decided to manipulate and force them into playacting in silly outfits. And why? For the sake of money! Cats have rights too!'

Some of the other protestors had heard Wanda speaking. Now they chimed in and started a chant of *cats have rights too*. I made a couple more notes before pushing through the picket line to the studio. The first person I spotted was Laura Gleep.

'Rosie!' she declared. 'Thank goodness you're here! We need media attention on this.'

Didn't Wanda Gibson just say the same thing?

'They seem unhappy about the movie,' I said tactfully.

'Unhappy! They're terrorists! What are they, Rosie?'

I stared at her. 'Unhappy terrorists?'

'Monsters! Criminals! Opposed to the arts! Haters of Bergman! Scorsese! Kurosawa!'

Actually, none of those directors had been mentioned, something that I felt compelled to point out. 'They seem more displeased about the cats being dressed up,' I said. 'What are your thoughts about that?'

'Cats love to perform! They love dressing up. Come with me, and I'll show you.'

I trailed after her into the old sports centre. It looked like they were getting ready to film a scene. Sets had been built to resemble a section of roof, a kitchen window, and a back alley. No matter what anyone's opinion might be about the movie, the set designers had to be congratulated.

The lighting was impressive too. Most of the lights over the sets were off, but the 'sky' behind the rooftop scene was on, making it look like early evening. Above the stage hung a 'flown' truss—rigging from which key and fill lights hung.

'We're just about to film a scene where Mrs Charles—aka Delilah Claw—meets Bob—aka Sam Whiskers, for the first time.' She raised her voice. 'Can the cactors be brought in?'

'Cactors?'

'A word of my own making,' Laura confided. 'A combination of the word cat and actor. I'm considering trademarking it, particularly if Cat Burglar becomes the first in a franchise.'

Monica Crumb appeared with Mrs Charles curled up in her

arms. The woman arrowed over to Laura. 'Mrs Charles is most upset this morning,' she said. 'I made the mistake of sharing with her some social media commentary about the film. People were saying the *unkindest* things.'

'Critics!' Laura snorted. 'Ignore them, Monica. They always get what's coming! I ran into Les Dribbons at an event a while back. He'd given me a one-star rating for my movie, *Loving Lola*. I accidentally dropped a plate of seafood cocktails down his front.' She chuckled. 'Smelt of fish for a week, someone told me.'

'Mrs Charles is quite sensitive,' Monica said.

'She must be brave. And remind her of all the money you're, er, she's making.'

'That will help, although Mrs Charles has a creative soul. She acts for the love of it.'

Laura turned to me. 'See, Rosie?' she said. 'Mrs Charles acts for the love of it.'

I peered down at the cat in question. The black and white American shorthair wore a particularly grim expression.

Although it could have been offended by the social media commentary, I thought it more likely to be the cat burglar outfit she was wearing. It was a tight number in black-and-white stripes and a separate mask across her eyes. If I were dressed like that, I'd be unhappy too.

'I see,' I said, not really seeing at all.

'Anyway,' Laura continued. 'The show must go on! Where's Sandra and her little Bob?'

Sandra Shelby appeared with her red Persian, Bob. He looked a little happier, although he may have simply been in a better mood. Bob wore a miniature trench coat. I stared a little closer. He really did bear an uncanny resemblance to...

'Humphrey Bogart?' I said. 'My goodness. He's the spitting image.'

Laura nodded. 'Makes you believe in reincarnation,' she said. 'Humphrey Bogart: reborn as a cat.'

'And Bob's favourite movie is Casablanca,' Sandra told me. 'He's watched it seventy-eight times.'

My mouth dropped. 'Seventy-eight times?'

'Fortunately, it's my favourite too.'

'Uh, okay.'

Laura clapped her hands together. 'Come now, everyone,' she yelled. 'We've got a movie to make! Everyone in their places.'

Although keen to get going, I decided to wait and watch for a few minutes. As an entertainment reporter, I'd been to a lot of movie and television shoots over the years. They always took a long time to film anything, and a lot depended on the patience of the actors. Some were incredibly temperamental.

I wanted to see exactly how this 'cat acting' worked.

Fortunately, at least, that wasn't the case today. Both Bob

and Mrs Charles were put into their positions by their respective owners and managed to stay put. Laura explained what she wanted the cats to do. Essentially sit for a while, and then Mrs Charles had to stroll across the 'roof tops'. The dubbing would be added later.

Laura called *action,* and the filming began. Both the cats sat there looking at each other. Then Laura told Monica to call Mrs Charles. Monica had a cat-toy that she held out of camera view. She waved it in the air, and Mrs Charles crossed the rooftops exactly as required. Bob's job was to stay precisely where he was.

'...and cut!' Laura yelled. 'Excellent! That's exactly what—'

Which was when one of the overhead lights broke free from the rigging, plummeted to the stage and smashed into pieces only inches away from Mrs Charles.

21

'Good grief,' Todd said, taking out his notepad. 'This sounds like a cat-astrophe.'

'Is that an attempt at humour?' I asked.

'Yes.'

'Then it's a *very* poor effort.'

He'd arrived at the film set only a few minutes before.

Pandemonium had broken out after the light fitting had struck the stage. The cats had gone running. People had screamed. Monica Crumb had tried to scoop up Mrs Charles and had only succeeded in falling onto the broken light and cutting her arm.

And Laura Gleep had fainted.

Todd and I crossed to where Laura sat slumped, a hand across her forehead and miserably shaking her head. Her goth assistant, Tina Landry, was fanning her with a copy of the script.

'Disaster,' Laura groaned. 'This has never happened to me

before.' Her eyes angled up to Todd. 'Although, I'm beginning to feel a little better. Officer! Officer! Help me up. Oh, you handsome hunk of man, thank goodness our local constabulary has arrived.'

She swooned into his arms. Todd caught her and shot a glance at me. I managed to not punch Laura in the nose.

Good grief!

Todd steadied her, but she continued to grip his shoulder as she spoke. 'I have never had this in all my years of filmmaking,' she said.

'Can you tell me what happened?' Todd asked.

They moved to a nearby table where Todd took notes as Laura explained the chain of events. I glanced around the set. Tina was standing to one side, looking flustered and a little scared. The three cat owners stood protectively in a group together, clutching their respective felines.

Monica was frowning and shaking her head. Sandra, holding Bob, was chewing thoughtfully on a donut. Gerry Baxter, the owner of Terry, was looking on with almost an expression of amusement.

I wonder what he's thinking.

Elisa Crumb, Monica's daughter, stood behind the group, looking almost pleased. *What an odd girl.* She'd barely said anything when I met her. *Why does she look so happy?*

'Rosie,' a voice said from behind. 'We *must* talk!'

I stifled a groan. 'Regina,' I said. 'How did you get in here?'

'I'm the mayor,' Regina said, tossing back her blonde hair. 'It's a kind of superpower that allows me in anywhere. Now we must speak about the tragedy that has befallen Mrs Charles.'

'Tragedy?'

'Yes. Now that she's been crushed to a pulp, it means a role has opened up for little Buttercup.'

'Regina,' I said. 'Mrs Charles is fine. A little spooked, but fine.'

'She's not squashed to a pulp?'

'Not even a pancake.'

I assured her that, apart from being a little spooked, Mrs Charles was alive and well.

Regina's eyes swivelled to Monica and her cat. 'Well, that's...wonderful,' Regina said, trying not to look disappointed. 'I brought my little Buttercup along—just in case. Have you had a chance to speak to Laura yet?'

'About...?'

'About Buttercup being in the film! Rosie! Surely you haven't forgotten?'

Actually, I'd done my best to forget. It was a shame I hadn't also forgotten how to find the old sport's centre, or that Harry wanted me to cover this story in the first place!

'Regina,' I began. 'As I said to you before—'

'Rosie,' Monica said, pushing past Regina. 'May we speak?

It's imperative.'

'Of course,' I said, glad to be free of Regina. I mouthed a quick *sorry* to the mayor and made for an empty hallway away from the mayhem. 'What can I help you with?'

Monica, holding her cat tightly, looked about fearfully. 'It's about this attempt on Mrs Charles' life,' she said. 'It was no accident.'

'Are you sure about that?'

The woman nodded. 'I've spoken to the gaffer.' That was the person in charge of lighting. 'He checked the rigging over the stage. One of the clamps had been loosened.' Her eyes filled with tears. 'It's only because of luck...'

I gave her arm a sympathetic squeeze. Although I wasn't a cat owner, I disliked anyone harming animals. Just the thought of it made my blood boil. 'I'll look into it,' I promised. 'But Todd Parker is the police sergeant here. He's the expert.'

'He's already told me there's not much he can do. He says it's an occupational health and safety issue.'

I nodded. 'All right,' I said. 'I'll do what I can.'

Wishing her well, I tracked down the gaffer and asked him about the rigging. As he'd told Monica, someone had loosened one of the clamps. A rope had been tied to the truss to make it sway. A sudden tug on it made the light fall.

I thanked him and found a quiet corner to think. Although the attack seemed to be aimed at Mrs Charles, it was possible the incident was simply designed to stop filming. A dozen protestors were on the street outside. If one of them found their way onto the lot, they could have rigged the lighting. But how could they get past security? That was impossible. Except Regina had gotten past security, and she wanted her cat in the movie.

Surely the mayor of Cape Carson wouldn't have sabotaged the film?

At that moment, Sandra and Gerry appeared.

'Rosie,' Sandra said. 'Can we chat? We need to speak about this so-called accident.'

Gerry spoke. 'We're not happy to be blamed for causing it. The lighting rig is ten feet over the stage. I'm afraid of heights, so I couldn't have gotten up there, and Sandra—'

'—is not made for climbing heights,' she said, indicating her rather Rubenesque shape. 'True, both Gerry and I would like bigger parts for our felines, but that doesn't mean we'd resort to violence.'

I frowned. 'I'm not sure how many cats are in the movie, but surely the sidekick and the detective are big roles.'

'Yes,' Gerry agreed, hesitantly. 'But—'

'But Mrs Charles is the star,' Sandra pointed out. 'And there can be only one star.'

This sounded like the cat version of The Hunger Games. She and Gerry were denying any involvement, but I only had

Gerry's word that he had a fear of heights. A capable person would have been able to scramble up a ladder in seconds. And Sandra's somewhat bigger size didn't disqualify her from climbing a ladder.

I thanked them for their help and returned to my jeep with Trixie. I settled down behind the wheel. Either of them could be guilty, but Gerry's cat, Terry, wasn't even in the scene. It was Sandra's cat, Bob, who had been at risk. Would she have risked Bob's life to get him a starring role?

I turned to Trixie. 'What do you make of all that?'

She yowled and lay her head on the seat.

'I know what you mean,' I said. 'To make matters worse, all I get from Todd is cat jokes.'

At that moment, the policeman in question came across the carpark wearing a rather amused expression. I gave him a wave, and he angled over.

'Discover anything?' I asked.

He laughed. 'What is there to discover? A piece of lighting fell down. That's a health and safety issue.'

'So you're not too worried?'

'When I discovered that death threats were being made against a cat—no, I think my interest in this 'case' dissipated.' He rubbed his chin thoughtfully. 'Mind you, if that cat were to die under mysterious circumstances, it could be a *purr-fect* murder.'

I groaned. 'That's a terrible joke.'

'Really, Rosie,' he grinned. 'You need to work on that sense of humour.'

'I'm sure.' I glanced at my watch. 'Look, I've got to get back to the office. I'll see you later.'

'Okay. And we need to be grateful for small miracles. It sounds like the lighting fixture missed that cat *by a whisker*.'

He winked, a gesture that I decided to ignore completely. A few minutes later, I was back at the Gazette in the office that I shared with Jay Patel. He was a pleasant young man with black hair, dark brown eyes, and glasses. He glanced up from his computer.

'Hey stranger,' he said. 'It's been so long since I last saw you that I thought you'd changed jobs.'

'I have. I've become a cat whisperer.'

'Huh?'

After explaining the issues around the movie, I also brought Jay up to date about Alex Carlyle's death.

'And you've already tracked down the killer?' he said. 'That must be some kind of record—even for you.'

'We got lucky.' I told him about chasing up the numerous locations where Henry Sterning had stayed. 'Besides, he's still being sought by police.'

A ruckus came from the front of the building, and I heard Doris, the receptionist, deliver a cry of delight. 'Well,' she called. 'Someone's got an admirer!'

A moment later, a delivery woman entered the tiny room with a massive bunch of red and pink roses.

'Wow,' Jay said.

After taking delivery of the roses, I sat them down on my desk and checked the card. Much as I hoped they were from a certain police sergeant with an appalling sense of humour, I was destined to be disappointed.

'No!' I said. 'This is not right!'

'Not a secret admirer?' Jay asked, frowning.

'These are from Buttercup!'

'You know someone named…Buttercup?'

'It's a cat.'

'Right.' Jay, obviously deciding that I'd finally lost my mind, returned to his computer. 'Better get this story done.'

I picked up my phone and made a quick call.

'Rosie Ryan!' Mayor Regina Lynch said when she answered. 'I assumed you received Buttercup's little gift?'

'Little gift?' I said. 'The florist must have just sawn off someone's rose bush and wrapped it in paper. This bunch is huge!'

'I'm so pleased. Flowers aren't cheap these days.'

'If these are intended as some kind of bribe to get Buttercup into the film—'

'Bribe! Rosie, the words Regina Lynch and bribe never go together. I'm not that kind of girl at all. Buttercup and I felt it was time you were rewarded for all the good work you do in the community. And your grandmother, Nan. Another wonderful woman. Truly a shining light.'

'Well, the flowers are beautiful, but if you think I have any sway over Laura—'

'Of course not, Rosie. It's that I know you and Laura go back a long way, and a role may become available—'

'Laura and I aren't friends—'

'Just a small speaking part for darling Buttercup will do—'

'Dubbed voices are being used—'

'My goodness! Look at the time. Better get back to work. A mayor's work is never done. Bye for now!'

Before I could get another word in, Laura had hung up, and I was left staring at my phone. I glanced over at Jay, who shot me a big smile.

'Buttercup sounds difficult.' He gave a sudden grin. 'Some might even say *catty*.'

I eye-rolled.

Everyone's a comedian!

22

The following day found me interviewing a man who had contacted the paper saying he'd invented a perpetual motion machine.

'People have been working on this for centuries,' Bernard Daffman said. 'Think of it, Rosie. The energy crisis solved—and by an inventor from Cape Carson!'

'Oh, yes,' I said dubiously. 'Just think of it.'

I was sitting in Bernard's living room on Sixth Avenue. It was a room filled wall to wall with the interiors of televisions and radios, and computers. Taking pride of place amidst this chaos was a device the size of a hat box that looked like a carousel. Weights dropped into the top of the carousel, making it turn. Attached to this was a tiny generator that illuminated a feeble light.

Bernard pushed a button, and weights fell into the tiny cabins, making the carousel rotate. 'I'm almost there,' he said. 'Just a little more development, and I'll be done.'

'So what part isn't quite there?' I asked. 'Because it looks like you've got it attached to a battery.'

'That's the part I haven't quite got working.'

'If you disconnect the battery…'

'It stops,' Bernard admitted. 'I just need to take that extra step. I'm almost there, though. Should have it sorted in the next few weeks.'

I glanced around his little workshop. 'What's that?' I asked, pointing to an object that looked like an old slide projector with a nozzle at the front.

'A new design in lawnmowing.'

'Really?'

'I'll show you.'

Bernard scooped up his device, and I followed him to his front yard. He positioned the invention on the footpath and pointed it at a patch of particularly long grass. After making a few adjustments, Bernard pushed a button.

Nothing happened.

'Um,' I began. 'Is something—'

A spurt of liquid flew from the nozzle and onto the grass. There was a flash of light, and the liquid burst into flames.

I shrieked and leapt back as Trixie barked in panic. The blaze spread to the device, which toppled sideways onto the footpath. Bernard ran inside and returned seconds later with a fire extinguisher. He put out the fire.

Speechless, I stared at him as he shamefacedly put down the extinguisher.

'Sorry about that,' he said. 'It's supposed to gently singe the lawn.'

'*Gently singe the lawn? It's a flamethrower!*'

'A similar design, I admit.' He nodded. 'Actually, that's where I got the idea. Just needs a bit of finessing.'

Finessing my foot!

'Maybe I'll be featured in this week's edition?' Bernard asked.

'I don't think so,' I said, furious that Trixie and I could have been turned into Baked Alaska.

'Next week?'

'We'll see!'

Returning to my jeep, I was just about to leave when my phone rang.

'Rosie?' the voice said. 'Lachlan Carlyle.'

'Oh, Lachlan.'

I hesitated. What had Kim said? *He was giving you the eye!* I tried to remain professional. The poor man had, after all, just lost his father.

'This is a surprise,' I continued.

'Hopefully, a good one.' He paused. 'I understand there's a suspect in our father's murder.'

'The police have someone in mind. Why do you ask?'

'It's just that I was thinking a bit more about the man we spotted in the forest. I was wondering if he could have been Wesley Carn.'

'Who's Wesley Carn?'

'He worked for our father many years ago. There was some kind of falling out, and the man disappeared, apparently with a lot of money. Wesley was rather tall with glasses. The more I think of the man I saw in the forest, the more I wonder if it could have been him.'

'I can mention him to Todd.'

Lachlan hesitated. 'Actually, Rosie,' he said. 'I was hoping you might be able to look into this yourself. Maybe on the quiet.'

'Why?'

There was another pause before he said, 'It's a bit delicate. Maybe we can meet for a coffee? Or lunch? It might be a little easier to discuss this in person.'

We arranged to meet at Sandy's Diner, and an hour later, I was sitting in one of the booths waiting for him to arrive. Kim zoomed in the door.

'Hey you,' she said. 'I didn't know you were coming here for lunch. I would have joined you.'

'It's actually a business meeting,' I added, 'with Lachlan.'

Her eyebrows shot up. 'Lachlan?' She grinned. 'Exactly what kind of business are you discussing?'

'He's got an update on the case. Wants to share something with me. Now,' I continued more firmly, 'get your coffee and vamoose! I've got to focus.'

Still grinning, Kim got her coffee and headed out the door. At that moment, my ex-husband George appeared.

Sandy produced a couple of bags of takeaway food for him to take, but then he spotted me.

'Meeting someone?' he asked, arrowing over.

'Yes. It's a work thing.'

'Oh, then I won't hang around. Just wanted to check that you were fine with this marriage thing.'

I stared at him blankly. I'd been so busy over the last few days that his upcoming marriage to Sadie had momentarily slipped my mind. 'Fine,' I said hurriedly. 'Yes. Great. It's wonderful news.'

'Amanda thought you looked a little shellshocked.'

'It was a surprise,' I said. 'It's all fine. Now I'd better focus on this meeting.'

He smiled, grabbed his food, and headed out.

Great, I thought. *Peace at last.*

Todd walked in the door.

Good grief! Why didn't I arrange to meet Lachlan somewhere else?

'Rosie,' he said, crossing to my table. 'Grabbing some food?'

'Uh, yes.' I purposely glanced at my watch. 'It's a work thing.

The guy should be here soon.'

'Anyone I know?'

I felt myself reddening. 'Lachlan Carlyle.'

'Really?' Todd's face was unreadable. 'It's about the case, I suppose.'

'Yep.'

'By the way, I've looked into the inheritance issue of Alex's will.'

'Really?' Now he had me interested. 'Who inherits?'

'It looks like it's Simon. Alex Carlyle apparently changed his will as regular as you change the batteries in your clock. Everyone I spoke to said he pitted the three kids against each other, and it's true.'

'So Simon will get most of the estate?'

'Almost everything.'

'And the others?'

'Virtually nothing.' He paused. 'If Lachlan says anything interesting, you'll let me know?'

'Of course.' I glanced past him. 'Here he is now.'

Todd turned and gave Lachlan a friendly smile. 'I didn't expect to see you again so soon.'

'Just catching up with Rosie.'

Todd went to the counter, picked up his coffee, and left as Lachlan settled opposite me. 'Is he any good?' Lachlan asked. 'As a cop, I mean.'

'Very competent,' I assured him. We scanned the menu and ordered food. Although I was as hungry as a horse, I ended up getting a cheese and tomato toasted sandwich. Lachlan, being a health fanatic, ordered a salad sandwich. I made some small talk about his carpentry business until our food and drinks arrived. 'You mentioned someone named Wesley Carn?'

Lachlan nodded. 'Wesley worked for our father for many years,' he explained. 'He was eccentric. Kind of a genius. Helped develop the Wishart system, the program that took the company to the next level.'

'I read about it.'

I bit into my toasted sandwich.

Yum! All that cheesy goodness!

'After Wesley developed it,' Lachlan said, 'there was some kind of disagreement between him and my father over owner-ship rights. Wesley thought he was entitled to a percentage of the takings. My father thought differently.'

'Who was right?'

'My father—as much as I hate to admit it. Wesley developed the program while employed by the company, so any inventions he developed were owned by Carlyle Groceries.'

'And he went missing after it was developed.'

'He was furious,' Lachlan said. 'So I've been told. A lot of cash went missing too. Wesley swore he'd kill my father, although Dad never took it too seriously. A lot of people said lots of things, and it never led to anything.'

'You think the man you saw in the forest was Wesley Carn?'

'It's possible,' he said. 'That's all I'm saying. The man may have been biding his time for decades, or hiding and finally lost his mind. Who knows how a crazy person thinks?'

'The police are following up on someone named Henry Sterning.'

'I don't know that name. Wesley could be using an alias.'

'Why don't you want to approach the police with this information yourself?'

'There's already animosity from Wesley's family,' he said. 'I've heard along the grapevine that they still blame us over the inventory system. The last thing I want to do is bring the police down on them.' He shrugged. 'And I could be wrong about the guy in the forest. Why have the cops knocking on their door over a suspicion?'

'Okay. Do you have any contact details for Wesley's family?'

Lachlan did. The man's wife—Gilda—lived in Mortlake, a town about an hour's drive north of Cape Carson. He gave me her address, and I said I'd follow up. We continued eating while chatting about life in this part of the world. Lachlan finally surprised me with a question of a more personal nature.

'You're not married?' he asked.

'Divorced,' I said, managing not to choke on my coffee. 'Like half the population.' I added. 'And you?'

'The same. I met the perfect woman, but I wasn't the perfect man. It turned out he worked at her office, so she ran off with him. All I ended up with was a mortgage and three cats.'

I grimaced. 'Don't mention cats.'

'Don't like them?'

Sighing, I told him about Cat Burglar and the protests around using cats as actors.

Lachlan shook his head. 'I would have thought the cats would be CGI these days,' he said.

'I think the movie's on a budget—a *tight* budget—and CGI costs a lot of money.'

Lachlan's phone beeped, and he glanced at it. 'Uh oh,' he said. 'That's a nuisance. I'm working on a house in Ballarat. I should have rescheduled the meeting. Can you let me know how you fare regarding Wesley?'

I assured him I would. He kindly paid the bill and left while I slowly made my way out to where Trixie sat, tied up on the footpath. Setting her free, I knelt down and rubbed her back.

'Lachlan seems very nice,' I said. 'I wonder how he feels about me.' She rubbed her head against my knee. I thought about how his gaze had lingered on my face. There'd definitely been some interest. And that question about being married. It had to mean something! 'Oh, Trixie. What will I do?'

23

'Is this the place?' Kim asked.

'This is it,' I confirmed.

Kim had kindly agreed to come with me to visit Gilda Carn. The day had dawned bright, clear, and hot, and we'd driven for an hour through rolling countryside to reach her home. The woman lived in a tidy farmhouse on the outskirts of Mortlake.

A few alpacas grazed in one paddock. Fruit trees grew in another.

We got out of the car and approached the house. Before I could knock, there was a deep, frenzied barking and a pounding on the other side of the door. Yelling ensued, followed by a woman dragging the door open and staring at us as if we were Martians.

Gilda Carn had wild, greying hair and wore a long, flowing dress and floral-patterned shawl. Her necklace was a massive gold and emerald-green beaded thing that looked so heavy it could have been used as a weapon.

'Salespeople?' she said. 'I've got a gun handy for salespeople.'

'Definitely not salespeople,' I assured her.

Kim added, 'The last time I sold anything was home-made lemonade when I was six. I accidentally poisoned our next-door neighbour, Mrs Ridley.'

'Good,' Gilda said. 'Salespeople are one step lower than roaches.' She glanced at Trixie. 'Nice dog. I have a German Shepherd.'

She may have felt it necessary to point this out, as the dog at her side was so big that it could have been mistaken for a small horse. It gave a huge, throaty bark, and she pulled hard on a lead around its neck.

'Behave Tiny!' she said. 'They're not salespeople!'

Kim and I exchanged glances.

Tiny?

After introducing us, I told the woman the purpose of our visit. Her eyes narrowed at the name Alex Carlyle.

'I heard he was dead. Murdered, too. Well, I'm glad someone finally did him in. Suppose it was just a matter of time. He was a monster.'

Well, I thought. *There's no confusion about Gilda's feelings.*

She agreed to allow us inside to answer a few questions. As it turned out, she wasn't completely mad, just a somewhat eccentric artist. The entire house was filled with landscape paintings, many of them very good. The place smelt of oil paint and turpentine. Gilda put Tiny outside as we sat in lounge chairs, surrounded by dozens of paintings.

On one wall were photos of Gilda when she was younger. She was with someone who must have been Wesley Carn. He was a tall skinny man with black-rimmed glasses and thinning on top. I exchanged glances with Kim.

That's the same description as the man in the forest.

There were other photos of Gilda with a young baby and also with a young man.

'I've lived here ever since Wesley was killed,' she said. 'It's been my little home now for twenty years.'

Kim leaned forward. 'You're saying that Wesley was killed,' she said. 'We were under the impression that he disappeared.'

'That's the story Alex Carlyle and that horrible family have been telling for years. The truth is that Alex murdered Wesley and buried his body somewhere.'

'Can you tell us about Wesley's career at Carlyle Groceries?' I asked.

'Wesley was a genius. Maths and science. Some might say he was on the spectrum. People found him hard to communicate with because he was so often in his own head and unable to relate to others. He found it hard to get jobs.'

'He was qualified?'

'A double degree at university in maths and science,' Gilda said proudly and then frowned. 'Wesley should have stayed in academia. That's really where he belonged. Instead, he decided to work in the private sector, but got fired again and again. Not because he was a difficult person, mind you. Others just didn't understand him. He couldn't connect. Couldn't talk their language.'

'But Alex Carlyle employed him,' I pointed out.

'Alex Carlyle was driven by money. Pure and simple. And he didn't care about getting on with people or the niceties of interpersonal communication. He quickly figured out that Wesley was a genius, and he could use his genius to make him a lot of money.'

'This was the Wishart system?' Kim said.

'Alex named it after Wishart's Gate in Dundee, Scotland, a famous entry to the city from the East. The system was ground breaking at the time because it combined the sales and reorder system. It was even written in a computer language of Wesley's own design. An amazing achievement in itself.'

'Wesley was able to do that?' I said. 'That's incredible.'

Gilda shrugged. 'Like I say, he was a genius. He created the code, wrote it, and—' her face blackened '—gave it to Alex Carlyle. It was the biggest mistake of his career. Carlyle's business was going backward fast. Overseas firms with bigger development teams were making their own software—and they had easier access to foreign markets. If Wesley hadn't developed the Wishart system, Carlyle Groceries would have been out of business. Wesley should have taken the program and left. A dozen other companies would have paid him handsomely for it.'

'But Wesley stayed with Carlyle?'

'I suppose he felt loyal to Alex.' Gilda shook her head. 'And Alex could turn on the charm when he wanted. Alex could be pleasant, or he could be a bully. The richer he got, the less he needed to be nice to anyone. Wesley should have left. If he had, he'd still be alive today.'

'Can you tell us about the last time you saw Wesley?'

'I went through all this with the police at the time. Alex announced that there was going to be a family picnic. A select group of employees and their families were invited to attend. We went along. We didn't want to, especially Wesley. By that time, there was already some bad blood between Wesley and Alex.' She shook her head sadly. 'That was an uncomfortable afternoon. Alex sat on a big seat at the head of a table the whole time. It was like something out of The Godfather. All afternoon, people were trying to curry favour with him.

'But not Wesley. No. My husband had worked out what Alex was like. Wesley couldn't connect, but he didn't understand. He knew what an evil creature Alex Carlyle was, and he challenged him. Told him what he thought of him and his business. Wesley told him he deserved a percentage of the profit from the inventory system.'

'What did Alex say?' Kim asked.

'He laughed,' she said. 'Said Wesley was only an employee and would be treated like an employee. Said no one else would employ him because he was a weirdo. He said Wesley should have been grateful.' The woman swallowed. 'Can you imagine? Wesley should have been grateful when what he'd done was singlehandedly drag the company back from bankruptcy?

'In the end, Wesley stormed off from the picnic area. I tried talking to him, but he wouldn't even speak to me. I ended up staying behind like a shag on a rock. No one to chat to. I eventually went for a walk.' Gilda stared into space. 'It was by complete coincidence that I came across Alex talking on his phone later. He was standing near the river, and I overheard him. All of a sudden, Alex said to whoever was on the phone *murder isn't always wrong*.'

I swallowed. 'Those were Alex's words?' I said. 'Exactly?'

'*Exactly*,' Gilda confirmed. 'I eventually caught up with Wesley and told him. Although I was scared, Wesley said we had nothing to worry about. He thought I was overreacting. Nothing happened for weeks. There was still bad blood, but Wesley had to get on with work. He had no other choice.' Her eyes misted over. 'And then Wesley went missing. He went into the office as normal. Worked late, as usual. The last person to see him was Elias Hill. He was in charge of development. Elias wished him good evening; that was the last time anyone saw

Wesley. My darling husband was never seen again. It was as if he had vanished off the face of the Earth. But I knew what happened. I knew.'

This was a lot to take in. Could Alex Carlyle have killed Wesley? 'Gilda,' I said carefully, 'There's something I need to mention. Alex's killer was spotted by several people. The man they describe fits Wesley's appearance—'

Gilda harrumphed. 'Rubbish!' she snapped. 'This was the Carlyle family, I suppose. You can't believe anything they say.' She clenched her fists. 'Even now, all these years later, they're still using Wesley as a scapegoat—'

The woman looked ready to burst into tears or scream. Trixie crossed and laid her head on Gilda's knee. The woman looked down at her. 'Dogs,' she said. 'Wesley bought me my first dog, Charlie. That was the first in a string of them. The only problem is that they don't live forever. In my darkest times, when everything seemed hopeless, there was always my dog. Now it's Tiny. He's the best friend I've got.' She looked up at us. 'I don't know if you can find Wesley. He's probably buried under a slab of concrete somewhere. But can I offer some advice on finding Alex Carlyle's killer?'

I nodded.

'Don't,' Gilda said. 'Whoever murdered Alex Carlyle did a good deed. They deserve a medal for murdering that man.'

24

We thanked Gilda for her time and returned to my jeep, where we sat in silence. The afternoon sun streamed through the windscreen as we stared at a plain of golden fields. A black crow settled onto a fence post, cried mournfully, and flew off.

'*Murder isn't always wrong?*' Kim said. 'I wonder who Alex was talking to.'

'I don't know. I doubt he was talking about destroying a hornet's nest.' The man I'd met was ruthless. Even I hated him. His involvement in murder wasn't entirely impossible. He may have wanted to kill the man who dared challenge him. Wesley Carn may have had a legitimate claim to the Wishart system. It would take a lawyer to unravel that.

But this raised another question.

'If Alex didn't kill Wesley—' I began.

'—then where's he been all these years? Hiding? How many years is it? Twenty? So he abandoned his wife and lived in seclusion before suddenly deciding to murder Alex?'

'It doesn't make sense. But there's another possibility. Did you see the photos on the walls? There was something that Gilda wasn't telling us.' I got out my phone and quickly started checking social media. It took a few minutes, but I finally got my answer. 'Here he is: David Carn.'

'Wesley and Gilda have a son?'

'Looks that way. It's telling that Gilda didn't mention him.'

'I think we need to pay him a visit.'

It took a few more minutes of social media stalking, but we eventually discovered that David Carn also lived in Mortlake. He was a locksmith in a tiny shop off the main road. After parking my jeep, we cautiously approached his shop.

Just as we reached the front door, a figure stepped out and pulled it shut behind him. The man, slim with glasses and thinning hair, clutched a brown paper bag.

Goodness, I thought. *He's exactly like the man who killed Alex!*

'Excuse me!' I called.

The man glanced at us—and ran.

Kim and I sprinted down the road in pursuit. The man turned the corner and headed up an alley between two shops. Although I was already falling back, Kim wasn't far behind, with Trixie ahead of her.

'Stop!' I yelled.

I really need to work on my fitness!

The man reached the end of the alley and raced diagonally across the road and down a narrow path between two buildings. By the time I reached the end, he was scrambling over a fence.

'Kim!' I gasped. 'Stop!'

My friend turned and waited until I caught up with her.

'Rosie,' she said. 'I can still catch up with him.'

David Carn was disappearing around the corner of what appeared to be an abandoned warehouse.

'And then what?' I puffed. 'I don't want you to get hurt. Or me.'

Trixie barked.

'Or you,' I told my beagle. I caught my breath. 'Cornering the man in a back alley is a great way for one of us to get injured. Come on. We'll round the building on the other side and see if we can find him.'

We followed a path around the warehouse. The old brick structure looked like it hadn't been used for years. Paint chipped off the sides, leaving a stippled pattern of brown freckles. Cobwebs spanned the dusty windows. The gutters on the roof were rusting and filled with holes.

We reached another alley. It had a building with a single locked door on one side and the concrete wall of another building on the other. Kim, Trixie, and I slowly traipsed down the alley and stopped.

'He's disappeared,' Kim said. 'Where could he have gone?'

Trixie whined at the door. I gripped the handle and gave it a shake. 'Trixie,' I said. 'This is locked. He couldn't have gotten through here.'

Wait a minute...

I knocked hard on the door. 'David!' I hollered. 'Come on out! We're not the police. We just want to ask a few questions.'

I knocked and called again. More silence followed, and then a rather sheepish-faced David Carn eased the door open. 'Okay,' he said. 'How did you know I was in there?'

'You're a locksmith. If anyone could have gotten through this door, it's you.'

'Can we talk?' Kim asked. 'I enjoy a run as much as anyone, but I'm not wearing the right shoes.'

'We can talk,' he agreed. 'But I refuse to be interrogated. I have rights.'

We returned to David's shop where he went behind the counter, leaving us on the other side.

Displays of blank keys covered the walls. Two key-cutting machines were built into the counter. There was also equipment for leatherwork repairs. It looked like he was a jack of all trades.

'Why did you run?' I asked.

'You took me by surprise.'

'I assume your mother told you about us,' I said. 'Otherwise, you wouldn't have reacted as you did.'

'She rang me. Said you were asking a whole lot of questions about my dad. Then you accused him of being a murderer!' His face reddened. 'Said someone who looked like him was spotted leaving the scene. The Carlyle family has a grudge against us. My father's genius made them successful—and then they killed him.'

'We didn't accuse your father of anything,' I said gently. 'Several witnesses described someone that vaguely resembled him.' *And you as well*, I thought, although I didn't say this. 'Your mother said he disappeared one evening after working late at the office?'

'He was murdered, and his body dumped. I was a kid at the time. You really need to talk to Elias Hill. He knew Dad well and what Alex Carlyle was like.'

'It's possible your father left of his own volition,' Kim pointed out.

David's face darkened. 'Left my mother?' he said. 'And me? He loved us. I know that. He wouldn't have run away.' He glared at us. 'Instead of blaming him, you should look at who benefitted from my father's death: Alex Carlyle and his family. They're utterly corrupt. You know my mother heard them talking about killing my father?'

'She heard Alex talking about killing someone,' I pointed out.

'And you don't think it's an incredible coincidence that my father died a short time later?'

'*Disappeared* a short time later.'

'So where has my father been all these years?' he challenged us. 'Living under a rock? And why would he surface now to kill Alex Carlyle? Why now?' David glared at us. 'You really haven't thought this through, have you? All you have is a description of someone—'

He stopped. The penny had finally dropped.

'Wait a minute?' he snorted. 'Me? *Me?* You think *I* killed Alex Carlyle?'

'Did you?'

'No.'

'Where were you Saturday night?'

'That's none of your business.'

'It's easier to answer us than—'

But David's patience was over. 'You can leave now,' he snapped. 'You're boring me with your stupid questions. If the police want to regard me as a suspect, let them. Now—*out!*'

Kim, Trixie, and I left, and David Carn slammed the door behind us. He didn't turn the shop sign back to *open*. Instead, he remained behind his counter, glaring at us as we moved away.

'Well,' Kim said. 'At least he's friendly.'

'He seems to believe that his father was murdered.'

'And that Alex Carlyle was responsible.'

We climbed back into my jeep. 'So that gives David motive for wanting Alex Carlyle dead,' I said.

Kim didn't speak for a moment. 'True,' she said. 'But we have the same issue again: why wait all this time to murder Alex? Why now?'

Neither of us had an answer for that. We drove back to Cape Carson. I was ready to eat, and I definitely needed coffee. As we reached the Diner, however, my phone rang: Harry.

'Rosie,' he said. 'Are you in town?'

'About to eat,' I said.

'Food can wait.'

No, it can't! I wanted to answer. *I'm starving!*

'Are you able to head over to the film shoot? Apparently, the set's been evacuated.'

Muttering under my breath, I promised I'd go immediately. Minutes later, Kim and I arrived back at the old sports centre. The protestors had dispersed, but most of the cast and crew were assembled in the car park. Kim and I pushed through them and found Todd speaking to Laura alone in the building.

'...must continue shooting,' Laura was saying. 'We've got a schedule to stick to.'

'I'm not sure that's safe,' Todd replied.

Laura spotted Kim and me. 'Rosie!' she cried. 'Darling! You must speak to your hunky police officer friend about closing down production. It's simply not possible!'

I turned to Todd. 'What's happening?'

'There's been a bomb threat,' he said. 'We got a call at the station a few minutes ago. Unidentified caller reported that a bomb was set to explode.'

Laura made a *ptash* sound with her mouth. 'That happens all the time,' she said. 'Rosie, you know that. You've been an entertainment reporter. There are always bomb hoaxes. Threats against entertainers. The show must go on!'

'Maybe,' I said. 'But Todd is right. People's safety comes first.'

Grumbling, Laura agreed that she would leave the sports centre. We started for the exit. At the last moment, she remembered that she had to retrieve her bag. It was sitting under her director's seat. As she grabbed it up, she gave a small cry and stopped.

'Laura?' I said.

The woman didn't speak, so Todd, Kim, and I hurried over.

'My bag,' Laura gasped. 'Look!'

We peered down. Padlocked to the strap of Laura's bag was a pink child's handbag.

'Good grief,' I said. 'Is that what I think it is?'

'You mean a bomb?' Kim swallowed. 'Like one that could explode at any second? I saw a horror film like this where the poor man ended up with no arms...or legs.'

'You mean he was killed!' I said.

'No. It was a horror film. He was *very* different after the explosion.'

Laura turned to her in horror. 'You mean...*this could be real? A real* bomb?'

'We need to evacuate this area,' Todd said. 'Rosie and Kim: out of here immediately. Laura—don't move.'

'I don't think it's real,' I said, staring at the handbag. 'Look. It's partly open and too small to hold explosives. And I can see paper in there.'

'Rosie—' Todd began.

I reached in and took out the paper. A single line of text was written on one side.

End this production—or else. This is your last warning!

25

'Rosie Ryan! You are the most irresponsible woman that I've ever met!'

I'd seen Todd Parker angry before, but it looked like I'd really annoyed him this time. We were sitting in his office back at the Cape Carson Police Station.

'It was obvious that the bag only contained a note,' I pointed out. 'And it was too small to hold any sizeable quantity of explosives.'

Now he looked like he really wanted to yell. 'Since when did you become an expert on explosives?' he demanded.

'Well,' I began slowly. 'There was a movie I watched last week. The bomb in it looked *very* big and had a red digital display. The handbag attached to Laura's bag had neither.'

Even to me, this sounded like the most pathetic excuse in history. Unfortunately, it was the only excuse I could think of at the time, and it also did nothing to calm Todd down. Actually, he made a strange strangling sound, and turned a bright shade of crimson as if trying to regain his self-control.

'Rosie,' he said, finally. 'You are going to get yourself killed one of these days.'

'I appreciate your concern. I will be more careful.'

As I'd already made this promise to Todd on at least a dozen occasions, he simply nodded. I thanked him and headed out of the police station with Trixie. Kim was waiting on the foot-path.

'How was Todd?' she asked.

'Fine.'

'So he was furious.'

I sighed. 'Yes. He was overreacting.'

'Rosie.' Now Kim looked annoyed. 'That bag could have exploded. You could have had your arms blown off!'

'Then my typing speed would have suffered.' What really irritated me was that both Todd and Kim were right. I'd been foolish to snatch up that bag. Anything could have happened, although I wasn't about to admit that to them. I hated it when I was wrong! 'Anyway,' I said, keen to change the subject, 'I need to get back to work.'

'Me too. We had a new girl start this week. I caught her trying to catalogue books about icebergs under mixer drinks.'

She decided to walk back to the office while Trixie and I drove back to work. I brought my notes up to date and actually finished work on time. Not long after five o'clock, I rolled in the door to find Nan sitting on the couch, knitting.

'You're home already?' she said. 'Don't you know that Dave and I could have been frolicking on the couch?'

'Then I would have been blinded for life.' There were things once seen that can't be unseen. I dropped my bag in my room, where I changed my shoes, before heading back to the lounge. 'I'm going for a walk.'

'Are you stressed?' Nan eyed me shrewdly. 'You look stressed.'

'Just a big day.'

'I heard there was some excitement over at that film set.'

I told Nan about the bomb threat and people disagreeing about the movie production.

'Animal welfare has to come first,' Nan said. 'Although, some of those cats do look kind of cute dressed up in outfits.'

I had to agree, although I wasn't sure how the cats felt about it. After telling Nan I wouldn't be long, I headed out the door with Trixie and walked to Cut Rock Lookout. The day was hot, and the air still. Although there were plenty of people in town, the lookout was deserted except for me.

The water was flat and calm, and the late afternoon sun glistened on it like a carpet of diamonds. The only break in the ocean was where a flock of seagulls were divebombing an unfortunate school of fish. Turning my gaze to the east, I saw surfers making the most of the waves along the length of Shelly

Beach.

Sighing, I settled onto a nearby bench. The last time I was up here, I'd been bawling my eyes out about George's impending marriage. Now when I thought about it, I realised I didn't care much about George getting remarried. It was his life, and Kim was right: a lot of water had passed under the bridge. He was allowed to do whatever he wanted, and I could do the same.

Other times, when I'd thought about moving on in life, it seemed like there were barriers in my way. For some reason, I'd thought back to my marriage to George and felt anchored to the past. I didn't quite feel that way now. I'd told Sandy Clementine at the diner that I'd been thinking about writing a mystery novel. Although I'd had a few false starts in the past, I now felt ready to commit to something new.

Trixie laid her head on my knee. 'Endings aren't necessarily bad,' I told her. 'What's that old saying about one door closing and another opening? Maybe I could be a writer. Other people have done it.'

She panted in agreement.

With a new spring in my step, I returned home and spent the evening with Nan. It wasn't until the following day, when I was back at work, that I began searching for Elias Hill. Once again, social media came to the rescue. It turned out that Elias was a keen astronomer, and his home address was listed as the contact for a club in the nearby coastal city of Warrnambool.

I stuck my head into Harry's office. 'I'm off to Warrnambool,' I said and explained what I was doing. 'Hopefully, it'll give me a clearer idea about Wesley Carn.'

'You think he could be responsible for Alex Carlyle's death? He could actually be this Henry Sterning?'

I shrugged. 'It's hard to say. I'm leaning more towards the son right now. He grudgingly spoke to Kim and me and then virtually threw us out of his shop.'

Harry raised an eyebrow. 'People weren't keen to see you and Kim?' he said. 'That's strange.'

'Don't be a smarty pants. People love us.'

'I'm sure they do.'

After growling goodbye to him, I went to my jeep with Trixie. Having Kim along would have been nice, but she had to work. Trixie and I drove down the coast, and we were soon pulling into the seaside city. Warrnambool was a beautiful place, bigger than Cape Carson, but still a community full of friendly people.

We navigated through the streets until we reached a small federation house on a quarter-acre block. The property had one of the best lawns I'd ever seen, bordered by rose bushes that looked like they'd been trimmed within an inch of their lives.

'That's one neat garden,' I murmured to Trixie.

My knock at the door was answered by a rotund man with a

big smile. 'You want to know about Wesley?' he said. 'Sure. I'm always happy to talk about him. He was the smartest person I ever knew.'

We trailed after Elias into a tiny house, the appearance of which matched the exterior. My home had never been this clean. It even smelt of bleach or something similar.

This usually would have filled me with a feeling of horror. After all, what strange person cleans when there are so many other things to do with your time? The only break in the perfect symmetry of the furnishings was the dozen images of stars and planets decorating his walls.

All perfectly lined up, of course.

'You're keen on astronomy?' I said.

'It was always an interest,' Elias said, settling opposite. 'Now that I'm retired, it's become a passion. I've been up at three in the morning more than once to catch sight of a comet or planetary alignment.'

I asked him about Wesley.

'The first thing you need to know about him,' Elias began, 'is that he wasn't like other people. He was different. These days, you might say Wesley was on the spectrum. He was a genius. Plain and simple. Could have been anything or done anything if he'd ended up in the right place.'

'But he worked at Carlyle Groceries?'

'Only because he couldn't get a job anywhere else. He was

impossible to get along with. Heck, I was his friend—maybe his best friend—and even I couldn't stand him half the time. He would insult me to my face. Call me a dummy. Said I was stupid because I couldn't see something that was blatantly obvious to him.' Elias shook his head. 'I didn't mind, though. There was no malice to it. Wesley thought pretty much *every-one* was stupid. The only people he would have gotten on with would have been Einstein and Hawking.'

'But you were friends.'

'Not at first. Then I realised he'd had a tough upbringing. Alcoholic parents and bullied at school. It was amazing Wesley survived at all.' He paused. 'Alex Carlyle could see Wesley was smart—and it made no difference to him that Wesley was odd. Alex knew he could make money out of Wesley, and that's all that mattered to him.'

'Wesley designed the inventory system?'

'Ground-breaking in its time,' Elias said, nodding. 'It's been superseded since, but it revolutionised the way that inventory was managed in independent grocery stores. It made millions for Carlyle Groceries at the time. Saved the company from bankruptcy, the truth be known.' He hesitated. 'No wonder Wesley was angry. He saw the company turn around, and all he got was a weekly salary and no thanks.'

'He wasn't entitled to a bonus?'

'Not the way the contracts were written. Anything *produced* for the company *belonged* to the company.'

'So Wesley was angry,' I said thoughtfully, 'and Alex wanted all the money for himself. Gilda believes that Wesley met with foul play. What do you think?'

'I don't know.' Elias hesitated. 'Alex Carlyle was a heartless man. Treated his children badly. Treated everyone badly. If he did—shall we say—dispose of Wesley, there could have been other reasons than the Wishart system. I distinctly remember Wesley saying to me that he knew where the skeletons were buried.'

I wonder what he meant by that.

'He didn't happen to mention where they were buried?' I asked. 'And whose skeletons?'

'No. Mind you, it's usually just an expression, but I think it meant something different when Wesley said it.'

'What do you mean?'

'Wesley gave a weird smile and said Jane knew about it.'

'Jane? Did she work at the company?'

'No. I pressed him on it, but he refused to say more. Wesley could be like that sometimes. Partly, it was his strange way of communicating, although sometimes it was just him feeling superior to others.'

Jane?

'Have you ever met Wesley's son?' I asked.

'David? He came to visit me about a year ago. Asked me a lot of questions about his father.'

I paused. 'People caught a glimpse of the man who killed Alex,' I said. 'It matches Wesley's appearance, but it could just as easily be David.'

Elias hesitated. 'I wouldn't like to think that,' he said. 'David seemed like a pleasant young man. Works as a locksmith.' The man rubbed his chin. 'Although I hate to say it, he did seem angry. Furious, really, about his father's death. Maybe his mother's riled him up about it over the years. David did say something about getting payback for what had happened to Wesley.'

'Really?' That sounded ominous. 'How serious did he sound?'

Elias shrugged. 'I don't know,' he said. 'People talk. Say things when they're angry. Mind you, Wesley's been gone for twenty years, and David was still upset. Sometimes wounds fester. Anger can do that sometimes.'

'That's true,' I agreed. 'Does the name Henry Sterning mean anything to you?'

'Henry Sterning? I don't think so. Who is he?'

'The suspect in Alex's murder.'

'And the police think Henry could be Wesley?' Elias frowned. 'Wait a minute. I just had a thought.' The man went into another room, and it wasn't until five minutes had passed that he returned clutching a book. 'Sorry about that.'

He handed me a science fiction novel entitled *Martians on the Moon*. I stared at it uncomprehendingly until my eyes dropped to the author's name.

'Henry Sterning,' I read.

'He was Wesley's favourite author. An old nineteen-thirties author. Long dead, now. Wesley lent me that book just before he disappeared. I've been hoping all these years that he might return for it.' Elias bit his bottom lip. 'I'd given up. From what you've been saying, though, it's possible that Wesley is still around.'

I asked Elias a few more questions, but he was unable to add anything more to what he'd already said. At the doorway, he paused just before closing the door. 'I hope you can find out what happened to Wesley,' he said. 'We were friends of a kind. It would be nice to know what happened to him.'

I thanked him and returned to my jeep where Trixie settled into the seat beside me. It was hot in my car, so I put the windows down and turned up the air conditioning. I rang Kim and told her about my conversation with Elias.

'Henry Sterning happened to be Wesley's favourite author?' Kim said. 'That's fairly damning.'

'It does kind of point the finger at Wesley.' I stared out at the street where some children were playing. 'I don't suppose you can take some time off work?'

'I can make up a few hours in the evening if you have something in mind. Adrian and I were planning on heading out for a late dinner anyway. What did you have in mind?'

'I've got a lead on the case.'

'About Henry Sterning?'

'No. Jane.'

'You know who she is?'

'Better than that,' I said. 'I've got a pretty good idea *what* she is.'

26

I pulled up outside of a six-foot high chain mesh fence. It was late afternoon, and the sun was casting long shadows across the dry golden fields. The paddocks all around were overgrown with weeds, and the road was dusty and potholed. Obviously, the council didn't make it out this way too often.

'This is it?' Kim asked.

'This is it,' I confirmed. 'The home where Alex Carlyle grew up.'

The clue was to be found in the old man's upbringing. When Elias mentioned Jane, I recalled the research that I'd done about Alex's life. His first family home had been a run-down property in one of those tiny towns that dotted the Australian countryside. Peering out across the golden fields, I spotted a timber home nestled in a small gully.

'The town of Jane is so small that it doesn't even have a shop,' I said. 'In fact, there are only half a dozen homes.'

'And this is supposedly where the skeletons are buried,'

Kim said, peering out at the overgrown field. 'That's a lot of property to search.'

'We shouldn't take it too literally. It is just an expression, although we may find a clue.'

'Pointing to...?'

'Your guess is as good as mine.'

I started walking alongside the fence.

'Rosie,' Kim said, her voice rising.

'I know what you're going to say,' I interrupted. 'And I'm not breaking in.'

'He gets quite upset when we do,' Kim pointed out. 'And he mentioned something about arresting you the next time you did it.'

'The good news is that we don't need to.' I pointed. 'There's a hole in the fence just under that tree.'

We continued through the long grass, keeping an eye out for snakes. This was summer, and snakes liked nothing more than to come out and bask in the warmth. The biggest danger with snakes was surprising them when they were happily sunning themselves on a log or rock. They didn't take too kindly to being interrupted.

We reached the break in the fence. A limb had come off the tree and broken through the wire. I nodded to the broken branch. 'That break is still fresh,' I said. 'It probably came down in that storm we had a few months back.'

Ducking through the gap, we pushed on to the low-lying federation timber home. The grass was up to our knees, and we made a point of creating lots of noise to give snakes plenty of time to skedaddle. Soon, we met an overgrown driveway and followed this to the front porch. The house had obviously seen better days, although it hadn't been vandalised. The place was probably too remote for hooligans to find it.

The front veranda was in good condition, with a timber railing all the way across. We rounded the building and found an old eucalyptus had been dislodged in the same storm.

Although it was still standing, a branch had crashed through a side window.

'Yes!' I said, pumping the air.

Kim was less enthusiastic. 'I've never seen anyone look so pleased to see damage to someone's property,' she said. 'You're not going in there, are you?'

'It's not breaking in!' I told her. 'It's the same as the door being wide open.'

'It's hardly the same—'

'Now give me a leg up,' I interrupted. 'I can't quite reach this window sill.'

Muttering under her breath, she gave me a leg up to the window. I broke away some shattered glass before shoving the branch out of the way.

'Almost there,' I told her.

Kim mumbled something that sounded like *make it quick*. I pushed up what remained of the sash and heard a ripping sound as I tumbled headfirst into the room. *Arrghh!* My skirt was torn, and I'd only owned it for a week! Picking myself up, I stuck my head back out the window.

'I'm fine,' I told her. 'Although my skirt is a little worse for wear.'

'And you have a cobweb in your hair and something that looks suspiciously like a live spider!'

After much yelling, I drove out the marauder and managed to calm down a little. Then I took a look around the room I'd landed in. The chamber was completely bare, with timber floorboards and a high ceiling. The air was hot and stifling. It smelt dry but wasn't unpleasant.

Probably no one's been here for years.

I stuck my head outside the door. The hall ran in a straight line through the house from the front to the back. It ended at what appeared to be a combined living room and kitchen.

I listened hard. Nothing. Good. I didn't want a homeless vagrant unexpectedly appearing from nowhere.

Opening the front door, I saw Kim waiting anxiously.

'What?' I said. 'Everything's fine.'

'Technically, this is breaking in.'

'*Breaking in* means different things to different people.'

'Where do those people live exactly? Mars?'

'Now you're being silly.'

'You know what Todd said last time when he found you'd broken in somewhere?'

'He wasn't serious,' I forced a laugh. Actually, Todd was *very* annoyed. 'Now come in. The place is deserted.'

Kim entered and searched the house. It didn't take long. Although Alex Carlyle's later life may have involved building castles, the house he grew up in was a tiny two-bedroom place with little in the way of luxury. I'd been inside homes like this before. The kitchen was ugly, with built-in cabinets painted in pastel shades of green and yellow. The walls were plaster lined with high ceilings. The heat seeped in during summer and bled out during winter. They were horrible places and only slightly better than living outdoors.

We lingered in the kitchen. 'It's hard to believe that these cabinets were stylish once,' Kim observed.

'No wonder everyone was skinny back then. How could you eat surrounded by colours like that?'

A single laminated table sat jammed in the corner. There were no chairs, though. With the rest of the house already searched, there remained only one place to examine: the crawl-space in the roof. The trapdoor leading into the ceiling was directly over the kitchen, which was handy because it was also where the kitchen table was located.

As I climbed on, something scampered in the roof overhead.

Kim stared fearfully at the ceiling. 'That's the resident ghost,' she said.

'If it is, the ghost has claws like a possum.'

'Especially scary,' Kim muttered. 'Half-ghost, half possum.'

Now wasn't the time to discuss the possibility of a hybrid ghost haunting the roof.

I pushed up the trapdoor and cautiously stuck my head through.

'Rosie?' Kim said cautiously. 'Can you see anything?'

'Besides a bird's nest and possibly a possum home?' I said. 'No. Not really. The smell is horrible, although there are no dead people up here.'

I climbed back down.

'Well,' Kim said, clearly relieved. 'Let's go. Whatever skeletons Wesley was referring to are clearly out for the day.'

Feeling despondent, I reluctantly nodded. I'd hoped to find something linking Alex to Wesley's disappearance. Instead, all we'd found was an empty, smelly house. We left via the back door and paused on the small back porch. The field behind the house was as desolate as the ground before it. A tiny windmill sat broken and abandoned. Not far from it lay the remains of an old shed. Although Kim wanted to leave, I wasn't ready to give up.

I marched resolutely across the dry ground to the shattered

shed. The next few minutes were spent in a rather fruitless exercise as I picked through the scraps of flattened timber and iron roofing. The place had obviously been in bad shape for years. All it had taken was a good breeze, and the whole thing had finally come down. It could have even been the same storm that caused havoc at the fence line and the house.

Trixie had been burrowing near some rocks. 'Come on, girl,' I called. 'We're going home.'

She ignored me. 'Hope it's only a rabbit that she's after,' Kim said. 'Dogs and snakes don't mix.'

I crossed to Trixie and was about to pull her away when I looked closer at where she was digging. The rocks lay in a rough circle with a sheet of rusting corrugated iron among them.

'What is that?' Kim asked.

'Other than a holiday home for snakes?'

We carefully pulled the sheet to one side to reveal a deep hole. It had been a well; now, it was just a rather deep and dry hole in the ground. The bottom lay in darkness. We carefully peered over the side.

'I can't see anything,' I said.

'I'll try the light on my phone.'

Kim shone it into the gloom. It still didn't reveal a lot. I took out my own phone and snapped a few photos. I brought them up on my phone and examined the pictures.

'Spot anything?' Kim asked.

I was about to answer *no* when I made out a white shape.

What could that—

'My goodness,' I gasped.

'Rosie?'

I angled my head around to examine the picture before speechlessly showing it to Kim.

'Rosie,' she said. 'That's...'

'...a human skull.'

27

It was late in the day, and the sun was casting long shadows across the Australian countryside.

A specialist team from Police Search and Rescue had been brought in to work with a forensics team to recover the body. One group had arrived in a police helicopter with another by road. Cops from Cape Carson were also there to search the home and surrounding property.

Kim and I watched the proceedings from the front seat of my jeep. A lifting hoist was set up alongside the well with a screen around it. Then the human remains were lifted out and placed into a body bag. All the while, a kookaburra laughed from a nearby tree as if mocking the victim.

Todd strode over to my window. 'Looks like the man's been dead for several years,' he said.

'So it is a man?' I said.

'We've even been able to determine more than that. He had a wallet.'

Kim and I exchanged glances. Even Trixie sat up a little straighter.

'Let me make a wild guess,' I said. 'The man's name is Wesley Carn.'

'Rosie,' Todd began, 'you are right on so many occasions—'

'I know.'

'—but completely wrong this time.'

'Huh?'

'It's too early to make a formal identification, but the licence in the wallet says his name is Greg Barnes. I've checked his background. He's a career criminal. Break and enters, mostly, but a few serious assaults. Hasn't been heard of for twenty years. At a guess, I'd say that's how long he's been in the well.'

Kim frowned. 'But how did he end up there?' she asked. 'Assuming he didn't fall in by accident.'

'And that probably didn't happen,' I said.

Before we could follow this line of conversation, there was a ruckus by the side of the road and Simon Carlyle came storming across the field. He stared in horror at the proceedings before his gaze settled on me.

'What's happening here?' he asked. 'The police rang Jasmine at home.'

Todd explained that Kim and I had found the body in the well and notified authorities. The man's mouth fell open. 'That's...well...' he swallowed before turning to Kim and me.

His face reddened. '*So you were trespassing?*'

'A...a branch had fallen onto the fence,' I stuttered. 'I thought—'

'Then you thought wrong!' Simon snapped. 'You had no right to intrude. This is private property.' He turned to Todd. 'I demand that these women be arrested!'

'That's not necessary. I was just trying to help—'

'I don't care,' Simon said. 'Officer, I'm pressing charges.'

'Rosie,' Todd said. There was no mistaking the glint of pain in his eyes. 'You and Kim go and wait at my car.'

'We were only trying to help,' I told Simon. 'Lachlan asked us to investigate.'

'He didn't give you carte blanche permission to trespass on our properties.'

As much as I wanted to protest, Simon was right. Lachlan had suggested I investigate. Not march onto people's properties as if they were my own. And both Todd and Kim had warned me repeatedly about breaking into people's homes, and I'd ignored them.

'Interestingly,' Todd went on, 'it doesn't seem to be Wesley Carn.'

Simon's face fell. 'It isn't?' he said.

Todd explained the man's suspected identity.

'I see,' Simon said, hesitating. 'Possibly, I was overreacting.' He turned to Kim and me. 'I'm sorry, ladies. It's been a trying time. Jasmine and I have also been planning a trip for the whole family on our boat. It's so we can all take a break.'

'That's all right,' I said, seeing an opportunity to make good our escape. I turned to Todd. 'We'll talk later.'

Kim, Trixie, and I scooted back to my jeep. Once we got there, Kim buried her face in her hands. A wheezing sound came from her.

Oh no! I thought. *What have I done? Kim is going to hate me!*

'I'm sorry,' I began miserably. 'Kim, I didn't expect—'

She dropped her hands—and burst out laughing as tears streamed down her face!

'Kim?' I said, bewildered.

She could barely stop laughing. 'I don't believe it!' she said. 'We're *not* getting arrested!' Kim was laughing so hard she could barely breathe. 'I thought we were going to jail!'

'So did I,' I admitted. 'I...I didn't mean—'

She held up a hand as she struggled to speak. 'It's fine,' she said. 'I'm just so relieved! I'm a free woman! I thought I'd have to get tattoos and fight the other prisoners. Maybe knife someone named Shark or Killer.'

'Kim,' I said gently. 'We would have been held overnight in the Cape Carson jail. And I've never met anyone named Shark or Killer.' I thought. 'Although I once met a drummer named Vomit who played in a heavy metal rock band.'

It took Kim a good couple of minutes to recover. 'There's something I don't understand,' she said. 'Why did Simon let us go?'

'I know. Simon changed his mind once he discovered it wasn't the body of Wesley Carn.'

I was about to continue when my phone rang.

'Rosie!' Laura Gleep cried. 'We've had a disaster! You must come immediately!'

'Really? What's happened?'

'It's Mrs Charles! She's been kidnapped...er, catnapped. Please come and help!'

I groaned but agreed. 'All right,' I said. 'I'll be there shortly.'

Kim rang up Adrian and told him she'd be late meeting him for dinner. It was after six by the time Kim, Trixie and I reached the sports centre. By then, it appeared that almost everyone was gone.

Laura Gleep met us at the gate. 'Rosie!' she said. 'It's a disaster! An absolute disaster!'

'Can you tell us what happened?' Kim asked.

'Monica and Elisa left Mrs Charles in her trailer,' she said. 'When Elisa returned later, she found the trailer had been broken into, and Mrs Charles was gone.' Laura flung a hand to her chest. 'This is terrible! Terrible.' Her eyes narrowed on me. 'What is it?'

'Terrible,' I muttered, although I didn't really think so.

Maybe I was feeling horribly uncharitable, but the kidnapping of a cat hardly compared to our other investigation. At the same time, I was here now, and both Monica and her daughter were probably distraught. I know I would be if anything happened to Trixie. 'Can you take me to see the others?'

'Of course. I need your help, Rosie. The police have shown a complete lack of interest.'

'Really?' Kim said.

'Oh, some dolt-headed constable turned up. He asked a few questions before saying Mrs Charles had probably wandered away. But that's ridiculous! The trailer was broken into and her cat carrier was gone!'

Laura led us around the side of the building to where the trailers were sitting. We weaved through the maze of temporary structures until we reached the one where Mrs Charles had been. A small window near the front door had been shattered. Glass lay on the ground outside, and the door was open.

The interior had been ransacked, and clothing, magazines, and paper had been flung all over the floor.

'This place appears to have been searched,' I said. 'What do you think they were looking for?'

'Money? Jewels? Who knows?' Laura gazed about. 'Oh! I just remembered!'

'What?' I said.

'Elisa Crumb saw the suspect! She saw him escaping!'

I wished Laura had told us this earlier. 'Where is Elisa now?' I asked.

We followed Laura to her trailer where an incredibly big group had been jammed into a tiny place. It was so crowded I would have thought some kind of world record attempt was being made.

Monica Crumb sat on a lounge, almost in a swoon, as Elisa fanned her with a manila folder. Tina Landry, Laura's personal assistant, was on her phone, presumably texting the news to social media. The owners of the other cats, Sandra Shelby and Gerry Baxter, were huddled together. They seemed to be doing their best to appear upset. At the same time, I noticed their cats—Bob and Terry—had both been groomed to perfection.

Ready to step into the starring role.

I crossed to Monica. 'I'm so sorry to hear about Mrs Charles,' I said. 'You must be quite upset.'

'Upset isn't the word I'd use.' The woman's eyes were glazed over. 'Mrs Charles has been my constant companion for years. I don't know how I can go on without her.'

Kim turned to Elisa. 'You saw the, uh, catnapper?'

'Yes.' The young woman nodded. 'I saw him escaping.'

'Can you show us which way he went?'

We followed Elisa back to the trailer. Elisa explained that she'd been returning to the trailer when she saw the man coming down the stairs. He'd caught sight of Elisa and scurried down the side of the trailer.

'What did he look like?' I asked.

'Skinny with brown hair and eyes,' Elisa said, thinking.

'And dressed?'

'Jeans and a t-shirt.'

'Colour?'

Elisa hesitated. 'White.'

'Can you show us which way he went?'

We followed Elisa through the maze of trailers. At the rear of the property was a hole in the wire fence, and beyond it lay a path through the bush. We continued onto this to a quiet road where a few lonely houses lined the other side.

'And what happened then?' Kim asked.

'The man got onto a motorcycle and rode off.'

'Was he the driver?'

'No,' Elisa said and stopped. 'Yes, I mean.'

Kim and I exchanged glances. 'This is really weird,' I said, deciding to take a gamble. 'Constable Turner related all this to us earlier. Fortunately, I know the owner of number fourteen.' I pointed to a weatherboard house. 'Lovely old lady named Margaret. She had a security camera installed after someone stole her letterbox. I checked the footage, and there's no sign of anyone driving a motorcycle in this street for days.'

Elisa paled. 'Really?' she said. 'That...doesn't make sense. I saw the man—'

'The mystery man who ran off at full speed around the trailers, carrying a cat carrier?' Kim said. 'And then scurried through the bush and somehow rode away on a motorcycle without dropping the cat.'

'I...well...'

Kim and I waited as the young woman's face went from white to red.

'That's...what happened,' Elisa struggled to speak. 'I mean...the camera at Margaret's home mustn't be working...that's the only explanation...'

'But we checked a second camera down the road,' Kim cut in. 'There's no sign of a motorcyclist on that one either.'

'I...'

'And let's not even go into that crime scene,' I cut in. 'Why would a thief toss the contents of the trailer if their goal was to steal Mrs Charles? And that glass was on the *outside* of the window? That clearly indicates that someone was already *inside* the trailer when the window was smashed.'

'No...I...there's no...'

'Elisa. *Please* tell us the truth. You've been behind all this from the beginning. The threats. The light that fell from the ceiling. The bomb hoax. And now the catnapping of Mrs Charles. Can you tell us why you did it?'

The girl looked ready to burst into tears. 'I haven't done anything...I mean...'

Kim spoke up. 'We want to help you,' she said. 'Tell us now, and maybe we can keep this quiet. If we speak to Constable Turner, there'll be a full investigation. The police will charge you with creating a public mischief. It's a serious offence.'

Now the tears tumbled down Elisa's face. 'I...I...it's my mother!' she wailed. 'She ignores me all the time, and I do *everything*! She loves that cat more than she loves me! I can't stand Mrs Charles! I hate her, and I hate my mother!'

'Elisa,' I said softly. 'Have you spoken to her about this?'

'I've tried! She never listens!'

'Then we'll speak to her,' Kim said. 'But first, you need to tell us about Mrs Charles. Is she alive?'

Elisa sniffed. 'Yes,' she said. 'She's hidden under the trailer. I was going to move her later.'

After returning to the office, we retrieved Monica and found a quiet room where we could explain what had happened. This led to a raging argument followed by tears, hugs, and finally, apologies.

'Does everyone need to know about this?' Monica asked, an arm around her daughter's shoulder. 'This is all my fault and never should have happened. I should have put my daughter first.'

'I think we can keep it quiet,' I promised. 'Let me speak to Laura. I won't go into specifics. I'll tell her that Kim and I used our investigative genius to solve the case in record time.'

Laura was ecstatic when I told her the good news. 'You and Kim are magnificent!' she cried. 'You've derived success from catastrophe!'

Or is that cat-astrophe? I wondered.

'There is one thing,' I said. 'I'd like to ask a favour.'

'Anything!' Laura gushed.

'Well, two actually.'

That night, just as I was climbing into bed, my phone rang.

'Rosie Ryan!' Mayor Lynch said. 'I owe you a lunch. No! *Several* lunches. Laura Gleep rang me this evening and told me she'd like to have Buttercup in the movie. A *starring* role, she called it. And she says it's because you put in a good word.'

'I'm glad I could be of help,' I said smoothly. I'd also arranged a speaking part for Kim as well.

'If there's ever anything you need, be sure to ask.'

I thanked her and hung up. Feeling satisfied with my efforts, I put out the light, lay in the dark, and closed my eyes. Within minutes, I was asleep. It wasn't until three in the morning that I woke again. I jolted upright in bed.

No, it's not possible, I thought. *That's too crazy.*

And yet it all made a sense.

Trixie woke and gave a tiny whine. 'It's okay, girl,' I said softly. 'I think I know who killed Alex Carlyle. The difficult thing will be proving it.'

28

I cast my gaze around the Carlyle Castle dining room.

Although I'd thought getting everyone together in one place would be near impossible, it was easier than I expected. The siblings—Simon, Lachlan, and Rani—were here, of course. Jasmine had come with her husband and now sat at his side, clutching Simon's arm with her eyes fixed on me.

Lydia and Elliot were here as well, despite looking terribly uncomfortable. They sat huddled together at the dining room table. Maybe it was the first time they'd ever been invited to sit there.

Sitting beside them was Allen Shipley. The doctor was frowning slightly as if wondering why he was here. He cast a curious glance over at the newcomers to the household: Gilda, her son David, and Elias Hill.

Todd was manning one door while Constable Turner stood at another. The only other occupants were Kim and Trixie. Kim shot me a quick smile of encouragement while my faithful beagle lay comfortably at her feet.

'This has been a strange mystery,' I said. 'Full of twists and turns and deaths over several years. It was difficult to solve, and then—as is so often the case for me—it all came together at once.'

Lachlan frowned. 'Simon told me about the body found on the property in Jane,' he said. 'You're saying that's part of this?'

'That man has been identified as Greg Barnes, a small-time criminal who did mostly break and enters. He disappeared over twenty years ago. No one knew until recently that he'd been offered a job that was supposed to make him a lot of money.'

'Which was?'

'He was hired to kill your mother.'

The mouths of the three siblings fell open. It would have been comical if not for the seriousness of the subject.

'He killed our mother?' Simon said stupidly. 'So he broke in...and...'

His voice trailed away as the truth struck home.

'Your father hired him,' I said. 'And then murdered Barnes after the job was done.'

Another shocked silence followed this revelation.

'That's...that's ridiculous,' Rani said, finally. 'Our father wouldn't do that.'

'There's no other explanation. Why else would his body be

in a well on that property? And Todd,' I nodded to the police sergeant, 'found a map secreted in his shoe detailing how to enter the house and when everyone would be out. Greg Barnes turned up at the house, murdered your mother, and made it look like a robbery gone wrong.'

'But why—' Jasmine began.

'Why have her killed?' I said. 'Carlyle Groceries suffered many financial ups and downs over the years. Todd looked into your mother's will. It seems she was insured for a substantial sum. I believe Alex Carlyle needed the money, and his wife's insurance would give him that.

'Greg Barnes was hired to murder Lucy when your father was scheduled to be out of town. This gave him the perfect alibi in case questions were asked. Once the deed was done, one final loose end remained: the assassin. Greg Barnes literally had control over Alex's future. I think he lured Barnes to that property to dispose of him—permanently.'

The three children seemed numbed into silence. They didn't know there was worse to come. It was Allen Shipley who finally spoke. 'What about Alex's killer?' he asked. 'The man we saw leaving the scene. Who was he?' He eyed Gilda and the others. 'I assume *you* have a good idea who killed Alex Carlyle.'

David's face reddened. 'What are you saying?' he demanded. 'We're sick of my father being accused of murder! If anything, Alex Carlyle killed *my* dad.'

'Rubbish!' Simon said angrily. 'Wesley Carn murdered our father. He broke in here and—'

A full-blown argument erupted between the Carlyle siblings and Gilda and David. Elias tried to defend his friend while Lydia, Elliot, and Allen Shipley exchanged glances in silence. Todd finally raised his hands to calm them down.

'This isn't getting us anywhere,' he said. 'Go on, Rosie.'

'Wesley Carn didn't murder Alex Carlyle,' I said. 'And I can prove it.'

Every eye in the room focused on me.

'Go on,' David Carn said.

'First, I want to go back to the night that Alex Carlyle died,' I said. 'Alex invited me for a specific reason; he told me someone wanted to kill him. Frankly, he believed it to be one of his own children.' I focused on them. 'He called it a 'portent of doom.' He asked me to keep my eyes open throughout the weekend. Usually, I would have declined such a request, but he practically blackmailed me into staying by promising a sizeable donation to our local hospital.

'Of course, Alex disliked the internet and mobile devices. Like everyone else, it meant that I had to surrender my device for the weekend. Although it wasn't easy, I did it. That night, Alex announced his intention to change his will—again,' I said. 'He'd done it so often that it had almost become a joke—except it wasn't. Not as far as the family was concerned.

Alex could easily cut Simon, Lachlan, and Rani from the will, leaving them comparatively penniless.'

'Rosie,' Lachlan said patiently. 'I'm hardly penniless.'

'True. As I say, it would leave you *comparatively* penniless. There's a big difference between a reasonable income and being rich beyond the dreams of avarice. And let's be honest. Each of you has made financial mistakes. Simon and Jasmine purchased real estate—and a boat—which has cost a fortune to upkeep. Lachlan started multiple businesses and failed. Rani's tried to succeed as an influencer, a hit-and-miss affair at best.'

I stopped, thinking back to the dinner. Like vultures, the family had sat gathered around Alex Carlyle's table, waiting and watching. And wanting.

'I awoke late that night,' I continued. 'It appeared that half the household was also awake. When I went downstairs, I heard a conversation coming from the library. It was Rani, although it was impossible to make out to whom she was speaking.' I gazed at her. 'Do you want to tell us why?'

Rani swallowed. 'I don't know what you're talking about.'

'You do. You were talking on a mobile phone.'

'We surrendered our phones.' She turned to Elliot. 'Isn't that right?'

The butler nodded.

'Rani, I'm sure you did,' I said. 'Or at least, you surrendered *one* of your phones. Despite your father's ruling, you still need-ed contact with the outside world.'

All eyes were on Rani, who finally shrugged. 'All right,' she said. 'I admit it. I had a second phone. So what?'

'What did you mean when you said *it isn't easy, especially when it's someone you've cared about*?'

'I don't know. It was nothing. Just a throwaway comment.'

'You knew your father's time was near, and you were already working out how to spend his money.'

Lachlan spoke up. 'Rosie,' he said. 'That means nothing. We have all thought about what we'd do with the inheritance.'

'Interestingly, you weren't up and about that night. Not until Simon fell down the stairs.'

'I'm a sound sleeper.'

I turned to Lydia. 'But I'm getting ahead of myself,' I said. 'You and Allen were speaking too.'

Allen spoke up. 'That's a private matter. Doctor-patient confidentiality applies.'

'Of course.' I stopped. 'Not that it matters. What matters is what happened the following day. We were gathered in the dining room when we heard Elliot at Alex Carlyle's door. Alex wasn't answering his knock. That's when we broke down the door. Upon entering, we encountered the ghastly form of Alex Carlyle. He was dead in the room with a knife jammed into one of his eye sockets: a grisly way to die. The only blessing is that it would have killed him instantly.'

Simon snorted. 'People don't usually recover from a knife to the brain.'

'It's an interesting method of murder,' I mused. 'Like so many other things in this case, it raises more questions than answers. A knife to the eye. Horrible. No one could gaze at him for too long. We quickly left the room and started down the stairs. On the landing, however, Jasmine spotted the killer disappearing into the forest.' I turned to her. 'That was most opportune.'

'I was lucky.'

'And you saw him for only a second.'

'Like I say,' Jasmine said, more firmly, 'I was lucky.'

'Rosie,' Simon said. 'If you're saying that Jasmine was some-how lying, then I should remind you that the killer was seen by several people.'

I continued. 'We all raced after the man. It was chaos, really, as we all charged through that stretch of forest. By the time we reached the road, the killer was gone. Apparently, he'd driven off, and we'd only missed him by seconds. Later, we realised that the killer must have escaped by leaping from one of the windows into the moat.' I paused. 'Although, there were things that didn't make sense. How did the killer get into the castle? The explanation was that several keys had gone missing over the years. He must have used one of those. Then we have the issue regarding the window in the servant's hallway. It had been open for half the night? If the killer arrived while it was raining, why did he leave the window open? What was he doing all that time? Then we have the locked room. How did the door leading from Alex's room onto the servant's stairs get locked? Who locked it? And the pool of melted rubber in the fireplace. What was it? Why did the killer feel the need to destroy it?'

'Who knows how a killer thinks?' Simon asked.

'Kim and I returned to where the killer had disappeared on the road and found a swipe card for the Kilkenny Arms, a hotel in Cape Carson. We went there and discovered that it was just one of three locations the killer—a man using the name Henry Sterning—was renting. Three places that he could work from.' I paused. 'It's a crazy idea when you think about it. Three locations means there's three times the chance that someone will see you. And yet, somehow, the killer had booked all these places using cash, and no one spotted him. Not even a glimpse.'

'He was hiding,' Lachlan said. 'A determined person can hide from sight.'

'It's a shame because it meant no one could identify him,' I continued. 'And yet the killer was spotted by so many people on the morning of the murder. Jasmine saw him and then Lachlan. And who else? Well, there was Rani and Simon, too.'

'And me,' Allen added. 'I spotted him as well.'

'Oh yes,' I said softly. 'You all saw him—and were able to provide a description. A man who looked like Wesley Carn, a man who had a motive to kill Alex. And what was found at the locations where the man had been staying? Books on programming and castles and maths. And the name—Henry Sterning—also happened to be the same name of Wesley's favourite science-fiction author. The only reasonable deduction would be that Henry Sterning and Wesley Carn are the same person.' My voice hardened. 'It was an open and shut case and utterly damning for Wesley Carn. The only hole in the argument was that no one could describe Henry Sterning. No one ever saw him. It even makes you wonder if Henry Sterning *existed at all*.' I paused. 'And yet how precise those descriptions were of the killer: tall with black-rimmed glasses, thinning hair, and slim build.' I glared at the group. 'And how similar. *Eerily* similar when you think about it. Every person who saw him described him in much the same way. It's rare when that happens.' I turned to Todd. 'Don't you agree?'

'It's incredibly rare,' Todd agreed. 'It's far more common to get conflicting reports.'

I studied the group. 'But in this case,' I continued, 'you all agreed. You described the same person, yet you only saw him for a few seconds.' I glared at Jasmine. 'You and Allen described him, despite being several hundred metres away.'

'What are you saying?' she demanded.

'Yes,' Simon snapped. 'What are you saying?'

'Let's put all this together,' I said. 'We have Wesley Carn, who provides the perfect scapegoat for Alex Carlyle's murder. We have a man who stayed at multiple locations with the same interests as Wesley Carn—who seems to *be* Wesley Carn—and yet no one ever saw him. We have a man that multiple witnesses saw leaving the crime. It only begins to make sense when you think of it as an enormous fiction.' I glared at the group. 'You didn't see a man leaving the castle because *there was no man.* Wesley Carn happened to be the perfect scapegoat.'

Several people started speaking at once, but I spoke over them.

'Simon, you were furious that Kim and I had discovered the dead body on your father's property—until it turned out not to be Wesley. Your whole attitude changed when it became obvious that it was someone else's body. Why? Because if the body belonged to Wesley, your story begins to unravel.'

Lachlan gave a hollow laugh. 'Rosie,' he said. 'You're an intelligent lady, and I respect you, but you're way off. Multiple people saw the man running away. And how do you explain Alex's murder? And the locked room?'

'It wasn't easy,' I began, 'until I remembered Alex's past. And what everyone said about him.'

'That he was a monster?' Simon snapped.

'No.' I stopped. 'That he was a *practical joker*. Everyone commented on the terrible pranks he would pull. Nasty pranks they were. He liked devices and tricks and things that fooled people. It didn't matter that people were harmed, whether physically or psychologically. Jasmine even suffered a knife to the face.' I shuddered. 'This got me thinking about what we saw after we broke down the door. It was a terrible sight. Alex Carlyle with a knife poking from his eye. It was horrible to look at—and so we didn't. We turned away as Allen examined the body and declared him dead. We got out of there as quickly as possible. After that, things happened very quickly. Jasmine and Allen saw the killer escaping, and we all pursued him.'

'That's what happened,' Allen said, his voice firm. 'We were all there.'

'Except Alex Carlyle was still alive.'

This was greeted with dead silence. And then—

'What?' The person who spoke was Lydia. She had been silent for so long that I'd almost forgotten she was present. Now the woman was staring at me in disbelief. 'You're saying Mister Carlyle was still alive?'

'Years ago, Allen came to Alex Carlyle's aid when he was sideswiped while crossing the road. Alex mistakenly came to believe that Allen could be trusted. The problem is that Allen's perspective changed over time. He saw the money that Alex had, and he wanted some of it.

'A carefully orchestrated plan was created because of Alex's 'portent of doom.' Alex had received a snake in the mail. Allen happened to be here at the time and came to Alex's rescue. It made Alex wonder who sent it to him and how he could discover who was loyal and who wanted him dead. He became convinced that it was one of his three children. But which one could it be?'

'This is ludicrous!' Simon snapped.

'I don't know who sent the snake to Alex. It could have been one of you, or maybe it was an old business associate. Either way, a plan was formulated to fake Alex's death. Allen and Alex decided to make it look like murder. A knife in the eye was a satisfying way to horrify people enough so they would not look too closely. Creating a fake knife and blood made from latex is no big deal. Not in this day and age. And the result was impressive. What Alex Carlyle didn't know was that he was unwillingly falling into a trap.

'You see, there'd always been a problem with Alex's inheritance. The old man played the siblings against each other. It was a no-win situation. Eventually, Alex would die, one would inherit, and the others would miss out.

'But there was a way they could *all* win. If the old man were murdered, they could split the inheritance between them. And no one would dare spill the beans about what really happened.

If one of them broke their covenant, they would all go to jail. Their blood pact would unite them. One person would commit the murder. The entire group would tell the same story: that they saw a man who looked like Wesley Carn escaping the crime scene.'

Elliot was shaking his head in amazement. 'You're saying Mister Carlyle was still *alive* when we entered the room?' he said. 'Mister Carlyle was just...*playacting*?'

'Exactly. That night, the killer met with Alex to put the plan into action. The phone line downstairs was cut and Alex was given the fake knife. What Alex *didn't* know was that the killer had made scuff marks on the opposite side of the moat. They needed to be there to support the idea that a killer had escaped by the window. After we saw Alex with that terrible injury, we left the room and went in pursuit of the mysterious man in glasses.' I paused. 'Except one person doubled back. That was you, wasn't it, Allen?'

'You're talking rubbish,' Allen muttered.

'Someone had to do the dirty deed, and it was you. You're the one person I didn't see in the forest. In fact, I didn't see you again until I got back to the castle. I assumed you'd gotten back just before me, but you hadn't. After we left the castle, you returned almost immediately. The old man must have thought he'd pulled the ultimate prank. Everyone thought he was dead.' I stopped. 'And this is what Alex had wanted. He wanted my impression of what I saw. I think that part was true. He wanted to know how the siblings reacted after his death. Were they grieving? Distraught? Or celebrating? He must have been looking forward to seeing the looks on our faces when we returned and found him restored to life.

'Except it wasn't to be.' I turned to Allen. 'You removed the latex knife, produced a real knife, and jammed it into his eye. The window overlooking the moat was already open. It had been opened hours before. Alex probably didn't know. Although you could have tossed the fake knife into the moat, that was dangerous. It could be found. *You had to destroy the latex knife.* It had to be destroyed because it was the *one piece of physical evidence* that could bring you all unstuck. So you built a fire and disposed of the dummy knife. After it melted, it didn't look like anything at all. Just a pile of goo.' I stopped. 'Of course, there was something you didn't foresee.'

'Which was?' Allen's voice was sour.

'While we were away, Alex wheeled himself to the back of the room and relocked the door leading to the back stairs. *Why not relock it?* he must have thought. The prank was almost done. All that remained was the denouement, the final revelation when everything was revealed to be a huge joke. Of course, after he *really* died, both doors leading to the back stairs were locked, accidentally producing an impossible mystery. No one guessed that the door had been locked by *the man who was supposedly dead.'*

'This is all very amusing,' Simon said, folding his arms. 'I don't suppose you've got any evidence?'

'That's right,' Rani sneered. 'It's a great story, but without evidence, it's nothing.'

Lachlan sighed. 'They're right,' he said. 'I don't see that you have anything other than a pool of molten rubber. And let's face it, that could be anything.'

'Partnerships in crime rarely work,' I said, ignoring them. 'Someone always breaks. There are always double-crosses. Right now, I'm sure some of you think the money will be shared five ways.' I paused. 'You don't know that only two people will ever receive that money. The night before the murder, I also heard someone in the garage. One of the speakers was Jasmine, although I couldn't work out the other person's identity.' I stopped. 'Now, however, I know.'

The woman's anger flared. 'Shut up!'

'You were speaking to Allen,' I continued, unabashed. 'The man with whom you've been having an affair.'

'What?' Simon stared at her in astonishment. 'That can't be true.'

'It's true,' I said quickly. 'And an accident has already been planned for you, Lachlan, and Rani.' They stared at me. 'Oh yes. This boating holiday that Simon and Jasmine have been planning. What did she say to Allen that night in the garage?

Accidents happen—especially at sea. What's funny about that? What could it mean—other than an accident has already been planned for the three of you.

'The only survivors would be Jasmine and Allen. By default, Jasmine would inherit everything and then marry Allen after a respectful period had passed.' I gave a humourless laugh. 'That old saying is true, you know. There really is no honour among thieves.'

There was a terrible silence while the tension built in the room. I'd pushed things as far as I could. Now I had to rely on human nature. That terrible sense of distrust that evil people have of each other. There was nothing at first. And then—

'You!' Simon screamed at Jasmine. 'I trusted you! We all trusted each other!'

'Shut up!' Jasmine roared.

'No!' Lachlan said. 'Don't—'

But it was Rani who finally brought them undone. 'I didn't want to be part of it!' Her voice was high and desperate. 'I thought they were joking! I didn't know they would really murder Daddy...'

29

The water rolled up and down onto Cape Carson beach. It had a soothing effect. Hypnotic, really. Children laughed and ran along the seashore. A dog barked. Seagulls soared overhead.

Although the sun lay low on the horizon, the day was still hot. The Bureau of Meteorology—the BOM—had predicted a heat wave for the next few days. I didn't mind. Summer was here, and I was going to enjoy every minute of it.

Kim and I sat on a park bench overlooking the coastal path. A lot had happened since the meeting at Carlyle Castle. Allen Shipley had been arrested for murder with Jasmine and the three Carlyle siblings charged as accessories.

Although the Carlyle inheritance lay in doubt now that several of the beneficiaries were no longer eligible to receive their bequests, at least the hospital would still receive its donation. To Alex Carlyle's credit, he had already completed that paperwork before his death.

'They were a rotten lot,' Kim said.

'Very nasty,' I agreed, patting Trixie. 'Money made them do terrible things.'

'There are still a few things I don't understand.'

'Only a few? You're doing very well.'

Kim laughed. 'Tell me about Elliot and his conversation with Simon when you first arrived.'

'Although Elliot and Lydia seemed like faithful servants, in Elliot's case, it was not quite as it seemed. Todd looked into Elliot's background and found he'd been arrested years ago for several drunk driving charges. There was a news clipping in Alex's belongings about a woman who'd been severely injured in a hit and run. It's too late now for anything to be done about it, but it seems fairly clear that Elliot was the driver.'

'So he was blackmailed into working for Alex?'

I hesitated. 'Let's just say Elliot was encouraged to remain there,' I said. 'Alex liked to control everyone around him, and that's how he controlled Elliot.'

Kim scowled. 'It knew butlers couldn't be trusted,' she said. 'And Lydia?'

'Lydia was always loyal to Lucy Carlyle. After her death, she transferred that loyalty to Alex, thinking he needed her help. It was foolish. I don't know what she thinks of herself now that she knows the truth.'

'So Alex Carlyle murdered the hitman who killed Lucy,' Kim mused. 'And what happened to Wesley Carn?'

I sighed. 'That's a good question,' I said. 'The poor man was obviously murdered by Alex. Sadly, the chances of ever finding his body are slim. My guess is that he's buried somewhere on that property. I personally think that David and Gilda will conduct their own search of the grounds in an attempt to find him.'

'You mean…trespass?'

'It's only trespassing if you get caught.'

For this illuminating view of the world, I earned a punch on the arm from Kim.

'Ouch!' I cried.

'You deserve that. One day you'll end up behind bars—and then what?'

'Then…I'll look at life from an entirely new perspective.' I thought for a moment. 'By the way, I've started writing my book.'

Kim frowned. 'Another book?'

'Hey, don't sound so negative. This is a murder mystery. I think I'm going to actually finish it.'

'So you'll be an author?'

'Is that such a strange idea?'

Kim gave me an appraising look. 'No. I can imagine you at book signings in the future.' She looked past me. 'Talking about the future…'

I followed her gaze to see a very handsome police sergeant

named Todd Parker walking his greyhound. Kim got up as they arrived. She said a quick hello/goodbye and virtually ran down the path as Todd settled beside me.

'Rosie Ryan,' he said. 'Have I mentioned what an irritating woman you are?'

'Once or twice. How have I been irritating on this occasion?'

'Breaking into that property in Jane. I said I'd arrest you the next time you pulled such a stunt.'

I stared at him. 'Are you arresting me?'

His eyes met mine. 'No,' he said. 'Actually, I've been wanting to say something to you. I heard along the grapevine that your ex-husband is getting remarried.'

'George? Oh yes. He's marrying Sadie.' I didn't sound or feel upset. Maybe I really had moved on. 'He needs stability, and Sadie's a nice person. She'll be good for him.'

'Great.' Todd looked at the water gently lapping the shoreline. 'So what will you do now? Now that his life has moved on?'

I burst out laughing. 'My life moved on years ago,' I said. 'I have dated, you know!'

'Really?'

'Yes! Hundreds of times! There have been several proposals, including a billionaire from London who wanted me to share his private island.'

'And you said *no*?'

'I didn't like his face.' I frowned. 'What are you trying to say?'

Todd hesitated. 'Sometimes I find it hard to say the words,' he continued. 'I get kind of tongue-tied—'

'Todd,' I said. 'What is it?'

He leaned forward and kissed me on the lips. It went on for a moment or an eternity. It's hard to tell. He pulled back and stared into my eyes.

'Was that okay?' he asked.

'I'm not sure. Maybe you should do it again.'

So he did.

The End

ABOUT THE AUTHOR

Darrell Pitt is a prolific author, with more than two dozen novels in print. Writing for both young and old alike, Darrell's books traverse multiple genres including cozy mysteries, science-fiction and adventure stories. A proud resident of Melbourne, Australia, Darrell shares his home with his wife and says he owns too many books (as if such a thing were possible!)

His literary journey began with a passion for crafting short stories in his youth, eventually evolving into full-length novels. Among his accolades, "A Toaster on Mars" earned a prestigious spot on the shortlist for the 2017 Russell Prize, showcasing Darrell's unique brand of humour. His novel, "The Firebird Mystery", received commendation from The Children's Book Council of Australia as a Notable book in 2015.

Darrell's Teen Superhero series has garnered widespread acclaim, while his Rosie Ryan books are a series of delightful mysteries set in a distinctly Australian environment. Among the books he's currently working on are a tech-thriller, a time-travel novel, and a mystery book set in 1960's Victoria.